A QUIET LIFE IN SEABURY

SEABURY - BOOK 10

BETH RAIN

Copyright © 2023 by Beth Rain

A Quiet Life in Seabury (Seabury: Book 10)

First Publication: 14th July, 2023

All rights reserved.

No part of this book may be reproduced in any form or by any electronic or mechanical means, including information storage and retrieval systems. Except for use in any review, the reproduction or utilization of this work, in whole or in part, in any form by any electronic, mechanical or other means now known or hereafter invented, is forbidden without the written permission of the publisher.

Published by Beth Rain. The author may be contacted by email on bethrainauthor@gmail.com

✽ Created with Vellum

CHAPTER 1

It was one of those spectacular summer days that made you feel glad to be alive. There wasn't a single cloud in the sky, and the waves were barely a ripple as they lapped at the shore of West Beach.

Lizzie Moore paused at the top of the stone steps that led down to the golden sand and stared around, doing her best to soak in every last drop of gorgeousness the day had to offer. It was only her third day back in town, and she felt as though she'd landed inside some kind of wonderful dream she never wanted to wake up from.

The soft air was rich with the tang of salty seaweed, and the gentle shushing of the waves was punctuated by the sharp cries of gulls as they swooped overhead.

Would she ever take Seabury for granted again? Somehow, she very much doubted it – not after spending such a long time away from her beloved hometown.

Brushing a stray wisp of hair from her cheek, Lizzie ran lightly down the steps onto the beach, where she promptly kicked off her Converse. Next, she peeled off her socks – wobbling around on one leg and then the other in her haste to feel the sand between her bare toes.

Lizzie knew she was in Devon, but this morning it was hard to believe she hadn't somehow parachuted onto a Caribbean island. It wasn't even nine o'clock yet, but the sky was an intense blue, and the clear water shimmered with an alluring, dazzling turquoise that almost begged her to roll up the legs of her dungarees and have a quick paddle.

'Maybe later…' she murmured to the sea.

Lizzie could feel the sun warming her skin through the sleeves of her black and white polka dot shirt. It was going to be a scorcher at this rate! Closing her eyes for a moment, she tilted her face to the sky and took in a long, deep breath. She knew she probably looked like a prize idiot, standing there with her eyes closed, grinning up at the sunshine… but she didn't care. She was so grateful to be back, she could practically dance a jig.

It was hard not to hold onto a great big ball of resentment towards her husband for taking her away from Seabury in the first place. Her *ex*-husband, she should say. After all, it was already five years since they'd separated, and Mark was re-married. Their two grown-up daughters had flown the nest years ago and were off doing their own thing. Lizzie, however, felt like she was only just finding her feet again.

Still, she was *happy* that Mark was happy. She was *grateful* he'd found someone who loved him. It was *wonderful* he'd been able to move on so quickly.

Hmm... okay, maybe the whole gratitude thing needed a bit more work when it came to her ex-husband – but at least she was trying!

Lizzie opened her eyes again, determined to enjoy the moment – rather than getting caught up in the past all over again.

'Look where I am!' she whispered to herself.

After more than a decade away, she was finally back in the one place that truly felt like home. She'd been brought up here – living with her lovely grandparents in their little cottage just below the town's allotments. When her nan had passed away and left the place to her, she'd happily settled there with Mark. Their two daughters had arrived in quick succession... and life had felt pretty much perfect for a little while.

Lizzie shook her head, doing her best to clear her thoughts as she wandered along West Beach. *This* was something it was easy to be grateful for. After years of living in a bustling, grubby city that had never quite made sense to her, she was home - and she never had to leave again.

'I am grateful. I *am* grateful...' she murmured as she made her way towards a group of old-fashioned, canvas deckchairs that were lined up facing the sea. They were picture-postcard-perfect – so cute and vintagey that they looked as if they'd graced the sands of West Beach every summer since the 1950s at least! She knew that was a clever illusion, though. They certainly hadn't been around when the girls were little... or when *she* was little come to that!

She came to a halt next to the nearest chair and ran her hand over the gorgeous blue, cream and pink stripes – trying to resist the urge to sink into its depths.

Just five minutes won't hurt!

Lizzie glanced around, searching for someone to ask permission from - but the sunny beach was deserted. She shrugged. No doubt someone would be along if they wanted her to move! She tossed her shoes onto the sand and flopped down into the chair with a huge, happy sigh.

What a glorious morning! She couldn't believe she had the entire place to herself! That was one thing you could say for Seabury – it did get a few visitors, but most of the tourists seemed to jam themselves into the larger resort towns further down the coast. They were probably all over in Torquay, Paignton and Dunscombe Sands right now, setting up their windbreaks and laying claim to their little patches of beach for the day.

Frankly, those other towns could keep the crowds... though, if it was always this quiet, it was hard to see how anyone in Seabury managed to keep a business going.

A little thrill of excitement mixed with anxiety ran through her. Was she mad, thinking she could make a life here? Could she really make her grand plan work in such a sleepy little place?!

'It has to work!' she said, settling back and letting her eyes drift closed as the usual sense of certainty hit her, just like it did every time she thought about the brand-new business she was going to get up and running now that she was finally home. She just needed to get the Old Grain Store tidied up, some stock ordered, a name chosen, some marketing underway…

'I am grateful,' she whispered again in an attempt to stop herself from mentally reciting her ever-growing to-do list.

Lizzie sighed, her eyelids fluttering in the warmth. Blimey, if she wasn't careful she'd be fast asleep before long. She was absolutely exhausted from the move.

Packing up her flat in Bristol had seemed to take forever – and now that she was finally here, she'd barely even started the unpacking. There were walls of cardboard boxes all over the cottage, and scarcely enough room to squeeze between them. She knew it would take a while to get around to emptying all the boxes – but she'd decided to focus on the shop first. Once the Old Grain Store was ready for customers, then she could focus on the cottage.

At least the place had been left clean and tidy for her. Lizzie had felt awful about asking Lou, her lodger, to leave. Lou had been completely cool about the whole thing, though, and it had all worked out for the best as Lou had ended up buying Seashell Cottage, just across the field.

In fact - Lou had made sure Lizzie had a smile on her face the minute she arrived at the cottage by placing a lovely card and bottle of wine just inside the empty hallway, ready to greet her the moment she opened the door. It had been such a wonderful surprise after the long and stressful journey. She'd opened the card, only to laugh out loud as she read the note inside - "Imagine I'm a Bunch of Flowers." According to the postscript scribbled underneath, Lou hadn't wanted to risk her arriving to a vase full of dead blooms.

Lizzie couldn't wait to meet her new neighbour. They'd chatted on the phone a couple of times, and she had a feeling they'd get on like a house on fire. In fact – she couldn't wait to meet everyone here! She was pretty sure a lot of the old faces would still be around... though it was unlikely they'd recognise her after all these years. She'd changed – a lot.

The last time Lizzie had lived in town she'd been a worn-out mum doing her best to wrangle two teenage daughters single-handedly because Mark had worked away more than he was at home. Now... well... she was definitely still worn out – but this time it was because she was busy chasing her own dreams for what felt like the first time in forever.

Lizzie gave a little shiver of excitement, then yawned widely. The sound of the waves and the cries of the gulls were telling her that at last, she could relax... at last, she was home.

∽

Lizzie frowned slightly as a shadow passed over the sun. She must have drifted off! She had no idea how long she'd been asleep... long enough for a cloud to appear, she guessed!

A gentle cough made her eyes fly open.

'Oh!' she said.

Oh didn't really cover it.

In front of her stood a man. She couldn't see his face because he was completely silhouetted against the sunshine, something that just served to outline beautifully strong arms, and ridiculously nice legs below a pair of cammo shorts!

'Erm, hi?' said Lizzie, trying to bring things into focus a bit better as she blinked and shaded her eyes.

'Hi!'

Ooh, he had a lovely voice too. Low and gravelly and... yum!

'It's a pound for the deckchair if you don't mind?'

'Oh... right!' said Lizzie, feeling slightly befuddled.

'Of course, hang about a sec... I know I've got some change here somewhere.'

She started to pat at the pockets of her dungarees.

'Here on holiday?' asked the man.

'No... no...' said Lizzie, completely distracted as she shifted onto one bum cheek to check her back pocket.

Ah Ha!

She triumphantly pulled out a handful of bits and bobs, only to find herself staring down at two clothes pegs, a couple of buttons, some hair grips and – randomly – a mint humbug.

How on earth did that get in there?

She peeped back up at the silhouette in front of her, doing her best to look apologetic, only to be met by a low rumble of laughter that made her bare toes curl into the warm sand.

'So... not visiting?' he said. She could still hear the laughter in his voice. 'Your first time in Seabury?'

'Nope. I lived here ages ago – but it's my first time back in about ten years.' Lizzie paused and sighed. 'Blimey, I seem to have lost a decade somewhere!'

'Happens to the best of us!' laughed the man. 'You must be Lizzie? Welcome home.'

'Thank you.' The words felt like a great big warm hug. 'Erm, how did you know...?'

'This is Seabury!' laughed the man. 'Anyway, see you around.'

He turned and started to wander off.

'Wait!' called Lizzie, trying and completely failing to

get out of the low chair. 'I've not paid you yet – and I *know* I've got some change in these blasted things somewhere!' she added, tugging at the dungarees' straps.

'I'll get it next time,' he said. 'And I'll do my best not to wake you up in future!'

'I was just resting my eyes,' chuckled Lizzie.

'The customer always knows best,' came the amused reply.

Lizzie watched the man as he began to walk away again, and she couldn't help but admire the view. Broad, solid back, muscular arms and tanned legs that were clearly very at home pottering around – barefoot - on the sands of West Beach. He was exactly the kind of guy who'd have had her heart racing when she was younger... but she was well past all that kind of nonsense these days.

Okay, so her heart *was* beating a little faster than normal... but it was probably just from the shock of being woken up by a random stranger. Or... maybe she was just hungry. Yes – that's all it was – and the sea air was probably getting to her too. She was still acclimatising to it – that was all. She'd clearly been in the city for far too long.

Lizzie fanned her face with her hand, suddenly realising that, like an idiot, she hadn't even managed to get the guy's name. Even worse – he already knew hers, so it would be super-awkward to ask in the future. She let out a long sigh. Was she *really* so out of practice at being a normal human being? It certainly seemed like it!

Ah well – she couldn't do anything about it now. The man was already a dot in the distance as he headed in the direction of the Pebble Street Hotel.

Right. It was time to get on with her day. As lovely as it was to be lounging around on the beach in a deckchair, Lizzie had work to do. But first – she needed to get her hands on a coffee… and maybe a sugary treat. Anything to help her get over the shock of waking up to such a glorious sight!

Grabbing her shoes, Lizzie briefly thought about pulling them back on but promptly changed her mind. Why bother? She wanted to feel the sand between her toes for as long as possible. Instead, she tied the laces together and slung them over her shoulder. Now all she had to do was figure out how on earth to get out of this chair without it eating her alive!

CHAPTER 2

After executing one of the least graceful manoeuvres of her life, Lizzie managed to haul herself back to her feet. Despite her best intentions about getting on with her day, she completely failed to resist the draw of a quick paddle. She rolled her dungarees up to her knees and let the gentle waves soothe her tired calves and feet.

When she eventually dragged herself away from the beach and was back on the pavement, Lizzie realised she had a choice to make. Unlike years ago, there were now several places she could grab her morning coffee. The fancy new cafe on North Beach had looked pretty funky when she'd driven past it the day before, but frankly, its cool interior was a bit too much like something out of her old city life for her taste.

As for the Pebble Street Hotel, memories of the miserable Veronica Hughes made Lizzie pretty hesitant about going anywhere near the place. Of course, there was a good chance that the old bat had moved on by this point, but just the idea of getting told off for being covered in sand and then force-fed the battery acid Veronica used to pass off as coffee made up her mind. That *wouldn't* be a positive start to the day!

That left The Sardine... and considering the gorgeous little place with its pretty, inviting yard was just across the road, Lizzie was more than happy with her decision!

'This is my life!' she murmured to herself, trying to shake off the feeling that she was just here for a visit and would have to head back to the drudge of the city at any moment.

This was *her* life. She could start every single morning like this if she wanted to – and no one could stop her!

'Morning!'

The café door opened just as she reached it, and the beaming face of an elderly gent appeared as he held it open for her.

'Lionel?' said Lizzie. 'Is that you?'

It certainly looked like the wonderful painter who used to live on the top floor of the hotel. The girls had loved to watch him paint whenever they bumped into him on the beach – and somehow he'd always managed to produce a little gift from his pockets for them – a new pencil each, or a bag of sweets to share.

'Well, goodness gracious me – if it isn't young Miss

Elizabeth!' he said with a smile that seemed to reach all the way up to his bristling eyebrows.

'You know it's always Lizzie to you!' said Lizzie, taking his hand and giving it a delighted squeeze as the rush of happy memories greeted her. 'And... I'm not so sure about young these days!' she added.

'Let's have none of that,' said Lionel. 'You look wonderful – I have to say, I approve of the dungarees!'

'Thanks!' said Lizzie, pushing away the temptation to bounce up and down in delight - she couldn't help but feel secretly thrilled. She loved them – even if Mark wouldn't have been seen dead with her wearing a pair of dungarees in public! Not that what he thought mattered in the slightest anymore!

'I wonder if I could talk Mary into getting a pair,' said Lionel with a decidedly naughty twinkle in his eyes.

'Mary?' said Lizzie.

'My fiancé!' said Lionel proudly.

'What? Wow!' said Lizzie. 'Congratulations!'

'Well, thank you,' said Lionel, still beaming.

'Sorry - I hadn't heard...' she started, realising her surprise was probably more than a little bit rude.

'Hardly your fault,' said Lionel, 'you've only just arrived back in town. There's an awful lot of Seabury gossip for you to catch up on.'

'More than ten years' worth,' sighed Lizzie.

For a brief moment, she felt a tug of sadness that she'd missed out on so many years here. So much had happened... so much life had flown passed... she couldn't help but wonder if the town would accept her as one of its own again. Maybe she'd only ever be a blow-in – someone who'd kept the house all this time without being an active part of the community.

With a frown, she gave herself a little shake, pulling herself together quickly. Now wasn't the time to be worrying about all that – not with Lionel watching her so closely.

'Don't you go worrying your head,' he said quietly, clearly reading more on her face than she'd said out loud. 'There are plenty of people around here who'll be delighted to fill you in. Give it a few days, and it'll feel like you never left!'

'Thanks Lionel,' she said, reaching out and giving his arm another squeeze.

'And how are the girls?' he said. 'I guess they've grown up a bit!'

'They're brilliant thanks,' said Lizzie with a fond smile, 'and hardly girls anymore – they're both in their twenties! Jenna's still floating around the world like the little fairy she always was. She's travelling around Morocco in her van at the moment.'

'And Megan?' said Lionel.

'Has her head down, working as hard as ever,' said Lizzie.

'I remember her serious little face,' said Lionel, nodding.

'Not much has changed,' said Lizzie with a sigh. 'I

swear she was born with a five-year plan in that head of hers.'

Lizzie adored both girls, but they were about as different to each other as it was possible to be. Jenna – her youngest - never seemed to have a care in the world. She danced through life and troubles just seemed to bounce off her as she went.

Megan might be the one with all the plans - five-year plan, ten-year plan, plan to pay off her mortgage and marry the decidedly boring Owen by the time she was thirty - but Lizzie wasn't convinced her daughter was quite as in control as she liked to think she was. Lizzie had never said anything, but she'd been half-expecting Megan to start coming apart at the seams for years.

'Right, I won't keep you any longer,' said Lionel, 'but give them both my love when you speak to them, won't you?'

'Of course,' said Lizzie smiling. She didn't want to burst the bubble of happy memories by admitting that she rarely spoke to either of them these days. Nothing bad had happened – it was just that Jenna was usually far beyond the reach of mobile reception or in a completely different time zone, and Megan tended to be at work or too busy planning world domination for idle chitchat.

Plus, there was the fact that if either of them needed a parent, it was *always* Mark they turned to first. Lizzie swallowed down the familiar edge of hurt. It didn't matter it had been *her* who'd been there every day – feeding, clothing, taxying and caring for them – she'd quickly become the invisible mum they could just take for granted. Mark got the calls for advice. Not her.

Lizzie shook her head. She didn't want to go there. Not this morning.

'Coffee!' she muttered, making her way into The Sardine.

'That – we can do!'

The smiling face that greeted her wiped every single uncomfortable thought from Lizzie's head.

'Ethel!' she gasped, hurrying to the counter.

'Hello Lizzie, lovely!' Ethel bustled out from behind the counter and wrapped her up in a huge hug.

'You look wonderful!' said Ethel, pulling back again and looking her over from head to toe.

'I was about to say the same!' said Lizzie with a laugh. Ethel hadn't aged a day since she'd last seen her. In fact, Lizzie was convinced that if anything, she actually looked younger.

'Well, that's what being in love can do for you,' said Ethel with a grin.

'Wait... what?' laughed Lizzie. 'Has the entire town fallen in love in the decade I've been away?'

'Pretty much!' chuckled Ethel.

'I just bumped into Lionel, and he said-'

'Oh yes – *quite* the to-do, him and Mary,' nodded Ethel.

'Do I know Mary?' said Lizzie, wracking her brains.

'I should think so,' said Ethel, 'seeing as you went to school here, and so did your little ones.'

'Mrs Scott?!?!' said Lizzie, her eyes wide.

'You'd better believe it!' laughed Ethel. 'Now *that* was a love story decades in the making. Not like my Charlie. That was completely out of the blue.'

'Charlie... Charlie Endicott? Up at the allotments?' said Lizzie, thinking hard as all the old names started to come back to her.

'That's him,' said Ethel.

'And how long has this little fling been going on?' said Lizzie.

'Ooh, a little while,' said Ethel breezily. 'And it's a bit more than a fling. He asked me to marry him!'

'Not you too!' laughed Lizzie. 'I go and get unmarried, and you lot do the exact opposite.'

'Something in the water in Seabury, to be sure,' said Ethel. 'You'd better watch out.'

'Nah – thanks all the same,' Lizzie snorted. 'I'm done with all that.'

'We'll see,' said Ethel raising her eyebrows.

'No – really,' said Lizzie, more forcefully. 'I want my life back. I never wanted to leave Seabury – and now, there's not a single soul on earth who can make me leave again.'

'Good for you,' said Ethel with a little nod. 'I'm just saying... when the right person comes along, it doesn't mean you have to lose the other things you love.'

'Don't get me wrong, I'm really happy for you – and

Lionel!' said Lizzie quickly before Ethel could go any further. 'But to be honest, I'm happy to spend the rest of my life having a torrid affair with Seabury, thanks!'

'Well – *that* I can understand,' said Ethel with a laugh. 'And how are the girls? I'm guessing all grown up by now?'

Lizzie nodded, grateful for the change of subject. 'Yup – they don't need me anymore – so I'm free to do what I want.'

'You're free... but the girls will always need you,' said Ethel, shooting her a soft look.

Lizzie felt her smile growing a bit tight. That had gone from one sticky subject to another in record timing!

'Let me get you that coffee!' said Ethel, clearly sensing her discomfort.

'That would be fab!' said Lizzie, glad to be on slightly less gnarly territory again. She took a deep breath. As much as it was lovely being in here, perhaps it was time to get back to work. Yes – what she really needed was to get busy bringing her new dreams to life. 'Any chance I could get it to take away?'

'Of course!' said Ethel. 'Anything to eat?'

Lizzie thought longingly of the pastry she'd promised herself for a moment before deciding that perhaps something a little bit more substantial might be a better choice.

'A sandwich, maybe?' she said doubtfully.

'We've got pretty much every filling imaginable,'

said Ethel, 'so there's bound to be something you fancy!'

Lizzie had a quick look down the long menu Ethel handed her and opted for bree and grapes along with a fancy salad before plopping down onto a chair to wait.

'So... do you own this place?' she asked, watching as Ethel pulled together various ingredients on the counter.

'Not me – I'm just holding the fort!' said Ethel. 'Kate Hardy owns it – you remember her, I'm sure? She's a bit younger than you I think...'

'I remember her,' said Lizzie. 'Lived with her dad?'

'Yes!' said Ethel. 'Lovely man. So sad she lost him so young. Anyway, Kate and her other half are on holiday. Sarah – that's our young superstar baker – is doing the last of her coursework this next few weeks so she's not around as much either.'

'Blimey – and here I was thinking this place was quiet,' laughed Lizzie.

'Rarely,' said Ethel.

Lizzie grinned at her. Well, that certainly boded well for her plans!

'Doesn't Lou who rented my house work here too?' said Lizzie

Ethel nodded. 'Yup – she's off on the sandwich rounds at the moment. She splits her time between here and Pebble Street.'

'I can't wait to meet her,' said Lizzie. 'She seemed so

lovely on the phone. I felt really bad about asking her to leave when I decided to move back.'

'Well, you mustn't!' said Ethel, wielding a vicious-looking knife as she chopped and sliced away merrily at the salad for her sandwich. 'She's happy as Larry in her new place – and I think being able to stay in your cottage was just the stepping stone she needed.'

'I'm so glad!' said Lizzie. 'She left me a gorgeous card, you know?'

Ethel nodded. 'She was desperate to leave you flowers too but she wasn't sure when you'd arrive!'

'Me neither!' laughed Lizzie. 'It took me way longer to pack than I'd been anticipating!'

'Always does,' said Ethel, adding handfuls of grapes to what was shaping up to be the biggest sandwich Lizzie had ever seen. 'Anyway, you're here now… you can take your time and settle in properly.'

'You're right,' said Lizzie with a happy sigh. 'You know, I can't believe Lou works for Veronica Hughes!'

'Ooh, you really *are* out of touch,' said Ethel, placing a fat paper bag containing her sandwich onto the counter before turning to fill a puck with coffee. 'Veronica's long gone. Lionel owns Pebble Street now!'

'What?!' gasped Lizzie.

'Yes… didn't he tell you?'

Lizzie shook her head, her eyes wide. 'No – he was too busy telling me about his engagement!'

'Typical Lionel,' laughed Ethel fondly. 'Well yes – he

bought the hotel, and his niece Hattie is head chef there. The food is wonderful – you'll have to try it!'

'Little Hattie who used to come down every summer holiday and cause mayhem?' said Lizzie, as an image of the wild little girl came to mind – always scruffy, always the ringleader.

'That's the one,' said Ethel.

'Blimey... and here I was thinking I could come back, safe in the knowledge that Seabury wouldn't have changed at all,' said Lizzie.

'Seabury might not have changed much,' said Ethel, 'but its people have.'

'So it seems,' sighed Lizzie. 'So it seems.'

CHAPTER 3

'Right, that's you all set, then?' said Ethel, handing over the biggest takeaway cup of coffee Lizzie had ever seen.

'I might be set for life with this monster!' she laughed, taking a sip and closing her eyes for a moment. She could almost feel the caffeine getting to work.

'Well… I'm guessing you probably need it,' said Ethel. 'Rumour is, you're going to be busy starting up a business?'

Lizzie's eyes flew open and she stared at Ethel in surprise. Was she just fishing or did she really know something? She'd barely told a soul about her plans for the Old Grain Store – she was far too superstitious for that. What if it all fell through?! There were several things she still wanted to get in place before she was ready to announce it to the world. After all, she didn't want to disappoint anyone – least of all herself.

Maybe Ethel was just fishing... but then again, that comment had been weirdly specific!

'I'm just a bit tired,' she hedged, hoping she might be able to escape without having to tell an outright lie.

'Well, maybe head home and put your feet up then?' said Ethel with a sly look on her face.

Lizzie grinned. Her old friend was clearly angling for more information, but right now she wasn't about to give in. Not yet. Then again, she did need to pick someone's brain about a few things, and who better to ask than Ethel?!

'I meant to ask,' she said, trying to sound innocent and unconcerned, 'does old Bob Jackson still do window cleaning?'

'No dear,' said Ethel. 'A young chap called Liam does that now – amongst other things. I can always ask him to pop around and see you if you'd like. Is this for your cottage... or the Old Grain Store?'

Lizzie had to fight the urge to gawp at Ethel's almost supernatural ability to gather information that simply wasn't available to the general public. She was going to *have* to tell her now, wasn't she?

Anyway, it wasn't like she was doing anything wrong. She'd bought the old building fair and square, and she was well within her rights to press it into service. She'd already jumped through all the hoops with the local council... ah... maybe that's where Ethel had been getting her information from! It was all meant to be confidential, of course, but she'd been warned that local set-ups could be about as airtight as a sieve!

'Yes – it's for the Old Grain Store,' she said, deciding to let Ethel in on that part of the secret at least. She'd keep the exact nature of her new venture to herself for just a couple more days… though she knew it wouldn't be long before it was all over town.

'Are you going to tell me what you're up to in there?' said Ethel with an air of amusement.

'Can I tell you in a couple of days?' said Lizzie, suddenly feeling like an awkward teenager rather than a budding businesswoman.

'Of course!' laughed Ethel. 'But if there's anything I can do to help, you know where to find me.'

'Thanks,' said Lizzie gratefully. 'Well, if you don't mind sending this Liam guy my way in the next few days, that'd be a huge help. The pigeons have made a right old mess. I mean – the windows are almost opaque – and that's just on the inside! I haven't managed to get the old wooden shutters open yet to see what the outside is like – that's a job for this morning. I sprayed the hinges with WD40 yesterday, but it's like the blasted things have been welded closed!'

'I'm not surprised,' said Ethel. 'They've probably not been opened up for about fifty years. After all, I don't think anyone's used the place for…'

'Decades?' laughed Lizzie. She'd certainly never

known it to be in use.

'It's been boarded up for so long, I don't think anyone around here even notices it's there anymore,' said Ethel. 'It's just part of the Seabury landscape... like the hills!'

Lizzie nodded. She could only pray that changed when she was ready to open her doors. She had grand plans for the old place... as soon as she'd finished evicting the spiders, sweeping up the pigeon poop and getting some light inside. With any luck, the town would welcome the change... though it wasn't exactly something the people of Seabury were known for!

'Don't worry,' said Ethel, clearly mistaking her frown as concern about the state of the windows rather than the magnitude of what she was undertaking, 'I'm bound to see Liam around later. I'll send him straight over.'

'Well... I'll be a bit busy this morning...' said Lizzie.

Her list of jobs for the day was so long, the last thing she needed was a curious stranger turning up and expecting a guided tour.

'Don't worry,' said Ethel. 'Liam's not likely to be free until late afternoon even if I do manage to pin him down. Anyway, it's due to rain in a little while, so he'll probably just stick his head in to arrange a time with you.'

'Rain? Really?' said Lizzie, turning to stare out of the café. It still looked pretty sunny out there to her!

'My Charlie's never wrong about the weather!' said

Ethel. 'He's good with things like that. You can trust him to know everything about rain... and potatoes. You mark my words - we're in for a downpour at eleven twenty-three.'

'Right – I'll bear that in mind!' laughed Lizzie. 'Thanks Ethel.'

'Don't work too hard!' said Ethel cheerily, waving her out of The Sardine.

~

Lizzie barely registered the walk along the seafront to the Old Grain Store at the far end of West Beach. In her head, she was busy running through the list of things she needed to do before she could even consider opening her doors. She had an electrician booked in a couple of days to bring in new wiring and lights... and she knew that would make all the difference in transforming the space into the image she'd been carrying around in her head ever since she'd started on this hair-brained plan of hers.

As lovely as it would be to put her feet up for a couple of days and enjoy being back in Seabury, she simply wouldn't be able to relax and enjoy it. For one thing, she wanted to be up and running as soon as possible. For another - she was simply too excited to rest! Sitting still for more than a few minutes when she had a dream to bring to life just wasn't going to happen.

Slurping her coffee, which seemed to be practically bottomless, Lizzie came to a standstill opposite the Old Grain Store and rested against the railings for a moment, staring at the building she'd lost her heart to. She was sure it just looked like a total wreck to anyone else, but to her – it was the start of a dream come true.

Constructed out of huge slabs of local, grey stone, The Old Grain Store boasted two of the most marvellous wide, arched windows that looked out over the sea. Right now, they were still covered with the heavy wooden shutters... or at least, what was left of them. Lizzie would have to do some repairs to get them looking their best again – but it wasn't just about prettying the place up! The shutters were the perfect protection against winter storms blowing up from the sea – and they wouldn't hurt when it came to a bit of added security either!

'Right!' said Lizzie, gearing herself up ready for action. She'd get those shutters open if it was the only thing she managed to achieve before lunchtime.

Jogging across the road, she balanced her coffee on the wide stone doorstep. She couldn't resist giving the shutters a quick yank before she went inside... it was always possible she'd simply not given it enough welly the previous day. Maybe the spray had worked its magic by now!

'Come on, come on!' she muttered, wrapping her fingers around the edge of the wood and pulling with all her might. It was no use. Just like she'd said to Ethel – they almost felt like they'd been welded in place!

'Fine. I'm bringing out the big guns!' she said, digging out the huge old key from her shoulder bag and unlocking the wooden double doors. Flakes of red paint coated her hands as she pushed her way inside, but Lizzie simply brushed her palms against her dungarees. She was on a mission!

'Now... where did I put that can?' she said, pausing just inside the doorway. As her eyes started to adjust to the gloom, Lizzie broke into a slow, wide smile.

Heaven. She'd somehow managed to land herself in heaven.

A delighted shiver ran right down her spine, and Lizzie hugged herself in a moment of pure joy. This knackered, dusty old stone barn full of pigeon poop and goodness knows what else was the start of something incredible... she just knew it!

'Right,' she said again, pulling herself together and wandering over to where she'd set up a makeshift workbench. It was probably the only thing she'd managed to get organised since she'd arrived – but she'd needed somewhere to set out all her tools. Well... *most* of her tools. There would be plenty more to come!

Lizzie scanned the selection, hunting for the little blue can.

'Ah ha!' she cheered, spotting it hiding behind the box containing her hand-held compressor.

Lizzie grabbed it and gave it a shake. Good – it was

still practically full. It might take the entire can to free those blighters up, but she'd have some daylight in here if it was the last thing she did today. Besides, if this Liam chap turned up, she'd need him to be able to actually *get* to the windows, wouldn't she?!

As an afterthought, Lizzie grabbed a lump hammer before hurrying back outside... just in case they needed a little extra *coaxing*. She liberally sprayed one set of hinges and had just turned to move over to the other window when she spotted an ominous bank of dark clouds marching across the sea towards her.

'Huh – maybe Charlie was right after all!' she muttered, raising her eyebrows. In that case, she'd better get on with it! If she was going to be stuck inside all afternoon, a bit of daylight would definitely be in order!

Lizzie quickly sprayed the hinges of the second set of shutters and then hurried back over to the first lot again, pocketing the can as she went. She took a firm hold of the ancient wood and gave it an experimental tug.

Nothing.

'Ah, come on you miserable git!' she growled. 'Fine... if that's the way you want it... you leave me with no choice!'

Lizzie grabbed the lump hammer. She knew it probably wasn't the best plan she'd ever had, but frankly, if she couldn't get the old things moving, she was going to have to cut them down anyway.

She'd just start light… nothing too full-on…

Lizzie tapped at the heavy, rusted metal right the way along the join. She did the same on the second hinge and then gave the shutter another tug. It shifted about a millimetre forwards, and then back again when she shoved it. Well, at least that was encouraging! She gave the hinges another, slightly more hefty tap or two with the hammer and then continued to wobble the shutter back and forth, easing it a little further each time.

Two minutes – and several more squirts later – and the shutter was open, leaving a little pile of rusty flakes on the pavement beneath it.

Not daring to stop for a victory jig, Lizzie quickly got to work on the other side, which didn't take nearly as long because she wasn't half as timid with the hammer this time. She was just about to head over to the second window when a large, cold drop of rain landed right on the back of her neck. In the time it took for her to turn around to eyeball the grumpy black clouds that were now almost directly overhead, the single drop had turned into a pelting curtain of rain.

'One window will have to do!' she laughed, bolting back inside just in time to hear the heavens open behind her.

Spinning on the spot to stare out at the downpour, Lizzie ran her grubby fingers through her already damp hair, then promptly cursed herself. Great – now she probably smelled like she'd washed her hair with WD40. Ah well – it was one of her favourite smells on earth, so why not! Besides, it wasn't like there was anyone else to be bothered by it, was there?!

Lizzie glanced down at her watch and grinned. She had to hand it to Charlie – he was spot on with his timing when it came to the weather forecast!

Glancing out through the curtain of rain again, Lizzie caught sight of a young couple on the other side of the road. They had their heads bowed against the rain as they dashed through the downpour, hand-in-hand. She could hear them giggling, and she couldn't help but smile.

Seabury really did seem to be full of loved-up couples... but that wasn't something that interested her in the slightest. Lizzie was done with all that nonsense. She would be quite happy here, tinkering in her new space and helping her customers.

A brief bubble of nerves surfaced as she wondered whether she'd really managed to make a go of this after all. What if there *weren't* any customers?!

'Don't be an idiot!' she said, rolling her eyes.

What she needed was a bit of positive action to get her back in the right frame of mind. Maybe it was time to do something symbolic.

Lizzie hurried over to her workbench and rummaged around until she found the old brass bell she'd brought with her. She'd bought it ages ago in an antique shop in Bath – hoping that one day she'd get to hear it go 'ping' the first time a customer entered her very own shop. She'd held onto the old thing for years, and it had become a talisman – a sign that she would make her dream come true... eventually.

Pocketing a couple of screws, Lizzie grabbed a pencil, her drill and a little stepladder. Sure – she was a long way from welcoming any customers just yet, but when she *did* finally open her doors, the little bell would remind her that she'd been brave and followed her dreams every time it sounded.

By the time she clambered back down the ladder, Lizzie was grinning from ear to ear. The bell certainly looked the part... now it was time to test it out.

She gave the door an experimental open and close, and couldn't help a *whoop* of pure joy escaping as a jaunty *ping* echoed across the Old Grain Store. It was perfect!

Now it was time to get back to a decidedly less symbolic job. There was nothing exciting or inspiring about the amount of pigeon poop she still needed to clear up before she could even think about bringing any stock in here!

Lizzie grabbed a broom and had just yanked an uncomfortable mask down over her nose and mouth when her newly installed bell rang out again. The unexpected *ping!* sent a shiver of excitement down her spine.

'Sorry!' she called over her shoulder, her voice muffled. 'I'm not open yet!'

'I can see that!' came a deep, amused rumble. 'I'm here about the windows.'

The voice was familiar...

Lizzie turned, dragging her mask back down.

Blimey!

'Hi!' she said, her voice several octaves higher than usual as she stared at the handsome face in front of her. She quickly cleared her throat. 'Hi!' she said again, this time at a slightly more human pitch. 'Sorry... erm... dust!'

'Right!' said the guy, quirking a grin at her. 'I'm Liam, by the way.'

'Hi!' she said again. Okay - that was her third *hi* in a row... what on earth was wrong with her?! Still, at least she knew his name now – because, of course, this was the same guy she'd met earlier on the beach.

Luckily, Liam didn't seem to have noticed that she was behaving like a total nutter. He was too busy staring around the half-cleared space, taking it all in.

'I'm Lizzie,' she said. 'Lizzie Moore.'

'Yes – I know,' said Liam, turning back to her with a grin that almost made her crumple to the floor in a jellified heap. 'We met earlier, remember? And anyway, Ethel told me. I have to say, it's lovely to see someone doing something with this old place.'

'Thanks,' said Lizzie. 'I've got quite a way to go yet, but I'll get there! Anyway – it'd be great to get the windows cleaned properly if you can fit me in sometime? I've only just managed to get the shutters open on one side so far – I'm afraid I was rained off midway – but I'll get the other one sorted out as soon as the rain stops.'

Lizzie closed her mouth, suddenly aware that she was gabbling. Why on earth was she feeling nervous? All she was doing was arranging for someone to clean the windows for heaven's sake!

'I can pop back tomorrow morning if that works for you?' said Liam.

'Yes please' said Lizzie with a nod. 'They'll need doing inside and out.'

Duh! Like that wasn't obvious!

'No problem,' he said with an easy shrug. 'And you're opening…?'

Lizzie wasn't sure if he was asking for the date, or angling to find out *what* she was planning to open.

'Soon,' she said with a smile she hoped was vaguely enigmatic rather than mildly deranged. 'Very soon.'

'Right. Brilliant,' said Liam, his eyes twinkling as he smiled at her. 'I'll see you tomorrow then.'

With one last grin in her direction, Liam ambled back out into the rain.

Lizzie reached out and put a hand against the wall to steady herself - she was feeling a bit weak at the knees, and more than a little bit dazed. What on earth was wrong with her? Probably just an overload of caffeine on an empty stomach. Maybe it was time to wash her hands and make a start on that sandwich!

CHAPTER 4

By the time she got home that evening, Lizzie was dusty, dirty, sweaty and exhausted. She was also happier than she could remember being in years.

She'd managed to clear the rest of the floor and had even made several repairs to the interior woodwork. Tomorrow, she would be ready to start painting and then... then it would be time to start ordering stock.

Shrugging out of her wet coat, Lizzie hung it on one of the pegs in the hall before doing a little jig of pure happiness. It burst out of her and she laughed at herself for being a total idiot.

The minute she stopped dancing though, a wave of pure exhaustion crashed over her. Okay – so it looked like she'd just used up her last scrap of energy. Tonight was going to be about putting her feet up and nothing else!

Lizzie edged along the hallway, squeezing between the two towering walls of boxes that were piled high on either side. She knew she really should spend a bit of time finding new homes for everything and unpacking a bit, but frankly, she was far more interested in getting the shop up to scratch first. She didn't mind living out of boxes for a little while and camping in the cottage. There would be plenty of time to get this place sorted out after the shop was up and running.

In any case, Lou had looked after the cottage so well that it had been immaculate when she'd arrived. That had made things a lot easier for her. At least she hadn't had to do a deep clean on top of everything else.

As much as she just wanted to flop down onto the sofa and close her eyes, Lizzie forced herself to head into the kitchen first. There was one thing she needed to do before she crashed out completely. She knew she should forage in her meagre supplies for something to eat – after all, the sandwich had been hours ago - but the bottle of wine Lou had left for her was singing a siren song right now!

Even though the cottage had been her home twice before – when she was a kid living here with her grandparents, and then again as a newlywed – it definitely didn't feel like hers yet this time around. It wasn't just the cottage either. Lizzie had a feeling that it was going to take a bit of time for her to readjust and relax back into the slower pace of life here in Seabury after such a long time away. She was more than ready for it though.

Taking a moment to lean against the kitchen sink and peer out of the window, Lizzie marvelled that this was *her* view - and no one could ever take it away from her again.

To be fair, it hadn't really been Mark's fault they'd had to leave Seabury. His job in Bristol just became more and more demanding – they'd needed the money but he'd started to resent the time away from his family. So they'd made the decision that it would be best for everyone to relocate to be nearer to his office.

The girls had been over the moon of course. Yes, it had meant them both finding new friends and getting used to new schools, but the thrill of living somewhere there was so much to do more than made up for it – for them at least. Lizzie had simply gone into mourning for her old life in Seabury… and had never quite managed to escape that feeling.

Well, she was home now – and she didn't need to hold on to all that sadness anymore. Lizzie blew out a long breath, focusing on the view.

The horizon was filled with grey clouds and a choppy, slightly grumpy-looking sea – and she couldn't imagine anything more beautiful. This was exactly where she belonged.

'Right!' she said, doing her best to bully herself into action. 'What on earth did I do with that corkscrew?!'

Flinging open one drawer after another, she finally

laid her hands on one - though she didn't recognise it. Maybe Lou had left it behind so that she had the bare essentials covered! She'd have to remember to thank her when she finally met the woman.

'Damnit!' she muttered. She might have a corkscrew in her hand, but there was no way she was going to sip her much-needed wine out of the coffee mug she'd used for breakfast. Or at least, not without a quick scout through a couple of boxes first!

Dragging her feet back into the hallway, Lizzie made a beeline for the first cardboard box marked "kitchen". Grabbing her house keys from the pocket of her dungarees, she used them to slice through the tape.

Opening it up, she rummaged through a bunch of cleaning products and roll upon roll of bin bags. Lizzie sighed, wishing she'd listened to the voice of reason in her head that had kept prodding her to label the boxes more carefully while she'd been packing. Unfortunately – that voice had sounded annoyingly like Mark – so she'd roundly ignored it!

Just as she was tunnelling through the fourth box in the stack – that was looking decidedly more useful considering she'd just unearthed a bunch of tea towels wrapped around various breakables – she caught the muffled sound of her mobile vibrating.

'Who on earth can that be?!' she muttered, straightening up.

Now, where on earth had she left that blasted thing? It definitely wasn't in the pocket of her dungarees, otherwise she'd have hit the roof! Maybe in her old fleece that was hanging over by the front door?

Clambering over the mess of boxes, Lizzie managed to yank the phone out of the fleece, scattering bits of oily rag and old cable ties all over the floor in the process. Just as she went to answer it, the buzzing stopped.

'Typical!' she sighed, eyeballing the screen to see if it had been anyone important.

Missed Call: Jenna

Before Lizzie even had time to wonder what miracle was at work to make her youngest call her from halfway around the world, the phone started to vibrate again.

'Jenna?' she said in surprise.

'Hey, mum.'

It was a terrible line – and Lizzie felt like she could hear every single one of the miles between her and her daughter.

'How are you, love?' said Lizzie. 'And... *where* are you?'

'Still in Morocco!' said Jenna. 'And not good. The van's broken down again.'

Lizzie rolled her eyes. This was nothing new. That van had been a liability from the moment her daughter had set off in it. Luckily, Jenna took after her rather than Mark. She was good at fixing things and didn't mind getting her hands dirty, so she'd managed to keep it limping along far longer than anyone had expected.

'Oh dear – so how long will it take you to fix it this time?' said Lizzie.

'It's dead this time, mum!' said Jenna.

Lizzie paused. She was pretty sure that was a wobble she'd just heard in her daughter's voice.

'Surely it's not that bad?' she said, hoping she sounded sympathetic rather than dismissive.

'Erm... there was a lot of smoke,' said Jenna. 'And... well... fire actually. After a mini explosion under the bonnet.'

'What?!' gasped Lizzie. 'Are you okay? You're not hurt, are you?'

'I'm fine. Really I'm fine...' said Jenna, though it was now obvious she was crying.

Lizzie swallowed hard. Jenna wasn't prone to getting upset about anything... so now she was really concerned!

'I rang dad but I couldn't reach him,' Jenna continued with a sob. 'He's probably off with that idiot wife of his... why's he never there when I need him?!'

Lizzie bit her lip and did her best to ignore the spike of hurt as it hit her in the chest. As usual, Jenna had gone to her father first. As usual, Lizzie was the backup solution. Right now though, none of that mattered. She just needed to calm Jenna down and figure out how she could help.

'I'm stuck mum, completely stuck. I've run out of money and I don't know what to do and I just want to come home!' Jenna's voice got higher and higher as her words tumbled out.

'Okay, love,' said Lizzie calmly, 'take a breath. We'll get this sorted out, don't worry!'

Lizzie listened as Jenna blubbed on the other end of the line, clearly trying to regain control of her sobs. Her heart felt like it would break at the sound. Her youngest had always been so independent and confident – a cheerful, bouncy child who'd turned into a beauty with the biggest case of wanderlust she'd ever come across. It was rare she ever asked for anything - and now, here she was, sobbing her heart out, clearly exhausted and completely freaked out.

'What can I do?' said Lizzie, injecting as much calm into her voice as she could muster. She needed Jenna to breathe and think as rationally as she could.

'I've got nowhere to go, mum,' she said. 'I really need your help.'

'Just tell me what you need, and we'll sort it out,' said Lizzie.

'Can I come home?'

'Of course,' said Lizzie, her heart melting at how young Jenna suddenly sounded.

'I promise it won't be for too long,' said Jenna quickly, the relief evident in her voice. 'I just... need to regroup. Then I can gather enough money for a new van and get going again.'

'We'll sort all that out when you're back,' said Lizzie, desperately trying to remain the voice of reason in the chaos, even though she was already wondering how on earth she was going to clear enough space between all the boxes to fit another person into the cottage. Still - it would be wonderful to see her daughter – if totally unexpected.

'Love – just to warn you, it's a bit chaotic here. I'm still living out of boxes,' she said, figuring it was only right to give Jenna fair warning.

'Mum – I've been living in the back of a van for over a year!' said Jenna with a slightly soggy laugh. 'It'll be like paradise, no matter what state it's in!'

Lizzie breathed out a sigh of relief. It sounded like the carefree, easy-going Jenna was back in charge again.

'Okay,' she said. 'Book your flights home and let me know when you need picking up.'

'Right,' said Jenna. 'Erm… mum… I don't have any cash.'

'Right. Right,' said Lizzie. She'd somehow conveniently forgotten that bit of the conversation. 'Well… okay…'

Lizzie rubbed her face, trying to muster enough brain power to figure out what to do next. Considering she'd just moved house as well as coughing up the cash for the Old Grain Store, she wasn't exactly rolling in money right now either. The savings she had left were set aside for the renovations and new stock.

She'd just have to figure that out, wouldn't she? Jenna needed her help – and that had to come first.

Besides, having her home for a little while would be wonderful. Not exactly restful... but that's what being a mum was all about, wasn't it?!

'Let me know how much your flight is going to be, and I'll transfer some cash to you tomorrow, okay?' she said. 'Enough to get you home, at least.'

'Thanks mum, you're the best,' said Jenna. 'But... can you do it now? I don't have enough left for food... or a taxi back to town.'

Lizzie let out a long sigh. It looked like that glass of wine was going to have to wait.

CHAPTER 5

*L*izzie yawned widely, bowing her head against the rain as she ambled down the hill towards town. It would probably have been more sensible to drive considering she was going to be decidedly soggy by the time she got to the Old Grain Store. But she was having a hell of a job keeping her eyes open - so there was no way she'd trust herself behind the wheel. Besides… driving would have entailed knowing where her car keys were… and that was beyond her this morning!

Even though she'd been exhausted when she'd finally fallen into bed the previous night, Lizzie hadn't slept well. She'd spent several nerve-jangling hours dealing with international money transfers – no mean feat with her patchy internet connection! Then she'd had to make sure that Jenna actually *booked* her flight home, rather than just ambling off to another country now that she had some funds at her disposal.

Not that Lizzie would have minded - but there had been something in her youngest daughter's voice that had troubled her - and she wanted to make sure that everything was okay before Jenna continued her nomadic wanderings. After all, there was only so much parenting she could do at one in the morning when the child in question was on an entirely different continent.

And now... Lizzie had her own issues to face. There was so much she needed to do to the Old Grain Store, but after bailing Jenna out, her next job had to be wrapping her head around the numbers and what they might mean for her grand plans.

Lizzie blew out an irritable breath as the weight of a bad mood settled on her shoulders. She was frazzled and exhausted... and now she was worried about money too. Suddenly, her triumphant return to Seabury didn't feel like the idyllic lifestyle choice she'd been hoping for.

Resisting the urge to head straight for The Sardine for a giant caffeine fix, Lizzie forced herself on through the rain. She'd have much rather stayed at the cottage this morning while she juggled her books, but at the last minute, she remembered that she'd arranged to let Liam in to clean the windows... and that meant unsticking the second set of shutters too!

How she was going to make it through the day

without a decent coffee was anyone's guess, but she was going to have to watch every penny for a little while... and that included treats from The Sardine. Who knew that last-minute flights from Morocco cost so much!

As she approached the Old Grain Store, Lizzie spotted a bucket of soapy water under one of the windows. Then, with a little flicker of gratitude, she noticed that the second set of shutters was open. Liam had clearly arrived early and worked a bit of magic... before disappearing into thin air!

Shrugging, Lizzie yanked the keys out of her pocket, keen to see what it was like inside with both the windows open and about an inch of dust washed away. She had just pushed the doors open when she spotted a man heading towards her through the rain.

Lizzie waved, and Liam did a kind of half-hearted salute, raising two takeaway coffee cups in greeting. He was clearly unable to say anything because he had a paper bag dangling from his lips.

Feeling her mood lift at such a welcome sight, Lizzie grinned and hurried towards him. As she reached out and took the paper bag gently from his mouth, something inside her fluttered - the action was strangely intimate!

'Morning!' said Liam, grinning at her. 'For some reason, I thought you might fancy some caffeine... and a pastry?'

'You might just be my favourite person in the whole

world right now!' she said, doing her best not to go weak at the knees.

'I don't know about that!' laughed Liam. 'But Ethel told me what coffee you ordered yesterday, and the custard pastries were fresh from the oven... so I couldn't resist, could I?!'

Lizzie unrolled the top of the paper bag, and the scent of still-warm pastries floated up to greet her, instantly dissolving the last remnants of her bad mood.

'Yum,' she sighed. 'Thank you – *and* for getting the second shutter opened too – that saves me a job!'

'No probs!' said Liam, handing her one of the coffees. 'A bit of brute force and ignorance did the trick.'

'That and the entire can of WD40 I doused it in yesterday!' laughed Lizzie.

Liam grinned and grabbed the bucket with his spare hand before following her inside.

'Wow – it's really made a difference!' said Lizzie, staring around, finally getting to see the space in the daylight for the first time.

'You wait until I've done the inside!' said Liam. 'You won't know the place.'

Lizzie watched as he put his coffee down on one corner of her bench, clearly eager to get straight to work. She knew she should do the same... but that didn't stop her from watching as he began to sluice down the inside of the old windows, the water quickly turning grey with decades-old dust.

It was completely mesmeric – maybe not the gross water, but certainly Liam's rhythmic movements as he worked, squeegee in hand, drawing filthy water away from the glass and turning the world outside crystal clear, one swipe at a time.

If only it was so easy to wipe away the worries that were swirling around in her head again! Lizzie sighed. It was time to head through to the little back room she had earmarked as a staff room. She needed to focus, and there was no way she could do that while Liam's decidedly toned arms were busy at work right in front of her!

Grabbing an old pencil and scrap of paper from the workbench, Lizzie hurried through to the tiny room which currently only boasted a wooden stool and an ancient table that rocked slightly.

Sinking down onto the stool, Lizzie took a fortifying swig of coffee and then – before she could chicken out - she started to jot down the depressing figures that had been dancing around her head all night.

It didn't take long before she was frowning down at a long list of numbers. This was even worse than she'd thought. Now that she had the hard evidence right in front of her, she couldn't ignore the truth of the matter.

After paying for the extortionate flight, along with the extra cash she'd sent so that she knew Jenna had enough in her account to keep her safe and fed until she got back to Seabury – Lizzie's precarious finances had now entered official disaster stage.

There wasn't enough money left for her to set up her business so that she'd be ready to open... at least, not in the way she'd planned. She might be able to stretch to about half the stock she had on her list... but there certainly wasn't enough for all the tools she wanted. There might be just about enough to cover the basic renovations the Old Grain Store still needed, but what good was a shop without the stock to fill it? And what use was a workshop minus the tools?

Had she really come this far, simply to be defeated by an exploding van in Morocco?

Lizzie dropped her pencil and sunk her head into both hands. There had to be a way around this... she just needed to figure out what it was. Not easy on so little sleep!

Heaving her head back out of her hands, Lizzie looked up only to find Liam standing in the doorway watching her.

'Sorry!' he said quickly. 'I was just wondering if you wanted me to do the windows back here too?'

Lizzie forced a smile and nodded. 'Yes please.'

'Okay. Cool.' Liam didn't move. He stood watching her for several long moments. 'Erm... is everything okay?'

Lizzie stared at him. She was desperate to have someone to share these worries with... but she'd barely told anyone about her plans for the Old Grain Store yet. Which was ridiculous considering she was planning on opening her doors in less than a month. Or... that *had* been the plan. Now everything was up in the air again, and there was a very real chance she might not be able to make this dream come true after all.

She desperately needed to talk to someone... and why *not* Liam. After all, he was standing there right in front of her and wasn't showing any signs of leaving her to it. Sure, the pair of them had only just met, but who else was there? Certainly not Mark... or the girls.

Liam *might* understand. One thing was for certain - she'd sat here in complete silence for long enough if his look of mounting concern was anything to go by.

'I want to open a bicycle shop,' said Lizzie. 'With bikes to hire, and a repair workshop too.'

She paused, not quite knowing what to expect now that she'd said it out loud. Lizzie wasn't really sure what she was waiting for – maybe for the sky to come crashing down, or for someone to start pointing and laughing. But Liam said nothing. There was no undermining smirk. No throwaway comment. He just stood there, patiently waiting for her to continue.

'Right,' he said when it became clear she wasn't going to say anything else. 'Brilliant idea - so... what's up?'

Lizzie shrugged and then cleared her throat. It didn't work. She still couldn't get any more words to come out.

'I remember you, you know,' said Liam quietly,

leaning his weight against the grubby door frame. 'As a kid, I mean.'

'You do?' said Lizzie in surprise.

'I went to school here too - just for a couple of terms. I stayed with my old aunt for a while and Mrs Scott let me join in with her lessons.'

'Oh wow!' said Lizzie, her eyes widening as the vague memory of a gangly, shy little boy rose to the surface. 'What were we then... about... ten years old?'

'About that,' said Liam with a nod. 'Anyway – I remember you. You were always zooming around on a bike... and when anyone's seat needed adjusting, or there was a puncture to be repaired, you were always the one to fix it! My chain came off once and I landed up in a hedge. You just whizzed over, pulled me out of the nettles – sorted out the bike and then zoomed off again.'

'I did?' laughed Lizzie.

Liam nodded. 'No one could keep up with you even though plenty tried. You were *so* cool - I don't think I even managed to get up the nerve to say thanks!'

'I'll let you off,' said Lizzie, feeling slightly dazed.

'Cheers!' said Liam. 'Anyway, if there's even the slightest hint of that awesome ten-year-old left in you – then I can't imagine a better thing for you to be planning!'

Lizzie smiled at him. He was right, of course – even her nan had called her Little Miss Fix-It when she was a kid. That's why her plans for this place had felt so much like a dream – it was her chance to embrace something that had always been a part of her.

'Erm... you're frowning again!' said Liam.

'Yeah...' sighed Lizzie.

'So it wasn't just a crisis of confidence then?' guessed Liam.

'More like a crisis of the wallet variety,' sighed Lizzie. 'I had everything worked out to perfection before I moved, but...'

'What happened?' said Liam.

'Daughter disaster!' said Lizzie with a weak smile.

'Now that's *definitely* something I can empathise with!' said Liam with a little smile.

'You've got daughters too?' asked Lizzie with interest.

'Just the one,' he nodded. 'And it's always... interesting!'

'I hear you there,' she laughed. 'I've got two girls. How old's your little one.'

'Definitely not little anymore!' said Liam with a wide smile. 'Mid-twenties.'

'Mine too,' said Lizzie. 'I'd love to say they're all grown up, but...'

'Not so much?' said Liam.

Lizzie shook her head.

'Amy is a junior doctor,' said Liam. 'She's probably more responsible than both me and her mum put together... but she's still my little girl, you know?!'

Lizzie nodded, though she couldn't help but

register a pang of disappointment at Liam's casual mention of his other half. But then, of course someone like Liam was taken. He was gorgeous... kind... good company... caring... and why did she care anyway? It wasn't like she was on the hunt for someone new – she already had more than enough issues to contend with.

'So... does Amy live close by?' she asked.

'Nah!' said Liam. 'She still lives with her mum up in the Midlands. Lucy's place is close to Amy's hospital, so that works out pretty well.'

'You must miss her?' said Lizzie, doing her best to ignore the fact that her treacherous brain started to shout *He's single! He's single!* on a loop.

'I do, but neither of us really see much of her, to be honest! She's always so busy.' Liam paused and ran his fingers through his hair. 'Anyway... that's enough about me. What's going on with your errant offspring... parent to parent?'

'Bit of a long story,' said Lizzie with a rueful smile.

'Isn't it always?' said Liam.

Lizzie nodded. 'Okay – so the highlights include an exploding van in Morocco and a deep-dive into the *bank of mum* to get back home.'

'Is this both the girls?' said Liam looking wide-eyed.

'Crikey, no.' Lizzie let out a long sigh. 'Megan wouldn't dream of doing anything so reckless as having fun. Anything that's not on her ten-year plan is left well and truly alone. No, this is my youngest, Jenna.

She's been travelling for ages and I think everything has just suddenly unravelled a bit.'

'Well... it's good you can help her out, I guess. So... is she moving back to Seabury to stay with you and your husband?'

'Husband?' Lizzie let out a loud hoot of laughter.

'Oh...' said Liam. 'Sorry... I just assumed... and I didn't want to listen to any local gossip.'

'Well, this time the local gossip is probably pretty accurate. The husband became an un-husband quite a few years ago now. It's just me. Just the way I like it!'

'Well... okay,' said Liam, ruffling his hair again. 'Erm – good for you. So Jenna...?'

'Yep – she'll be back with me for a bit,' said Lizzie. 'The cottage is still a total mess of boxes, but I'll sort it.'

'Right...' said Liam, still watching her closely. 'Right... but... that doesn't quite explain why I just found you staring at that piece of paper like the world was coming to an end!'

Lizzie smiled at him, grateful that he was pushing the point because she'd quite like to forget about the whole thing by this point. She might as well tell him the full story now she'd got this far.

'The money I just used to bail Jenna out was meant to be for this place – stock, tools, the hire bikes... I mean, I'll still get there eventually... I'm just trying to figure out how.'

Liam nodded and scratched his chin, looking thoughtful. Or maybe he was just bored. Lizzie took in a deep breath, instantly wishing she'd kept it all to herself. Poor bloke – he'd only come to wash her windows, not to run a therapy session!

'You know,' said Liam slowly, still rubbing his chin, 'I might just know someone who can help out.'

'You... you do?' said Lizzie in surprise.

'I'm not promising anything,' he said, 'but there's definitely someone you should meet. What are you up to this afternoon?'

CHAPTER 6

Lizzie stared at the wild, rambling hedges that lined the road on the way out of Seabury. Colours flew past Liam's van - a rush of lush greens dotted with the vibrant pink of Campions and the warm yellow of tall Buttercups. The rain seemed to have made everything brighter somehow, the colours more intense.

Cracking open the window, Lizzie took in a deep breath of air, sweet and heavy with the threat of more rain. She had to admit, she felt a bit odd right now. She was immensely uncomfortable about the fact that she'd somehow managed to commandeer Liam for the afternoon, ruining his plans in the process. At the same time, she felt relaxed and totally at ease in his company – which was a bit bizarre considering he was whisking her off to an undisclosed location with a vague promise of "knowing someone who might be able to help."

'Are you really sure you've got time for this?' she said, turning to him.

Liam flashed her a quick grin from the driver's seat. 'Seriously, will you stop worrying? I finished off my rounds this morning, and I only had a meeting with Ben planned for this afternoon – and he's already been called away to sort out someone's leaking toilet cistern!'

'Ben...?' said Lizzie, wracking her brain.

'He was at school the same time as Kate from the Sardine... and he used to hang out with Hattie whenever she visited Lionel. Ben and Hattie are an item these days!'

'Ooh, I remember my nan talking about him!' said Lizzie. 'Didn't he used to take himself to school in a boat or something?'

'That's him!' said Liam. 'Anyway, you need to know Ben – I'll make sure I introduce you. He's Seabury's handyman extraordinaire. Not that you need one, of course - but if you could ever do with an extra pair of hands, he's brilliant. He's always super busy though... so you can always ask me instead!'

'Thanks,' said Lizzie. 'So... do you guys work together?'

'Not yet,' said Liam.

'Sorry,' said Lizzie, 'I don't mean to be nosy... I just couldn't help noticing the bits and bobs you've got in the back of the van – it looks like you're ready for any eventuality!'

She'd actually been pretty jealous when Liam had opened the back up so that she could pop her bag in there. Sure, it was a total mess – but it was like a little workshop on wheels. He had his window-cleaning kit stashed to one side, and what looked like a couple of very well-stocked toolboxes piled up at the back next to a large mystery object under a tarp. Two or three deckchairs were stacked on top of everything else, awaiting a bit of TLC before any unsuspecting holiday-makers got themselves stuck in the broken frames.

'You know – you're going to have to be careful when Jenna gets here,' said Lizzie.

'Erm... why?' said Liam, looking bemused.

'This is exactly the kind of van she loves!'

'What, completely knackered?' he laughed.

'No, no!' said Lizzie, 'I meant she loves anything where she can just bung a mattress in the back before zooming off for another adventure!'

'She'd have a job getting all my stuff out first,' said Liam. 'I don't think I've completely emptied the back since I first got her.'

'Why would you when you've got it all arranged just the way you like it?' said Lizzie with a shrug.

'Exactly!' said Liam. 'Finally – someone who gets it!'

'So... if you don't work with Ben... what do you do?' said Lizzie. 'Other than the deckchairs... and the windows...?'

She couldn't help being curious about this guy

who'd just offered to whisk her off on some weird, magical mystery tour at the drop of a hat.

'I've got lots of bits and bobs going on,' said Liam. 'Seabury is a bit like that. Frankly – *I'm* a bit like that. I did try the whole steady career, nine-to-five thing for a while, but I hated it. I get bored quickly and I love to be outdoors… so I'm just building my life around that, really!'

'Why not!' said Lizzie. She loved his attitude, even if the idea of piecing together an income from lots of little jobs made her shiver.

'So yeah,' said Liam, 'there's the deckchairs - though that's just an excuse to hang around on the beach a lot. And then there are the window rounds a few times a week. I do some bits of gardening, and Ben and I might be teaming up too.'

'Doing what?' said Lizzie curiously.

'He's got requests for odd jobs coming out of his ears, and he's simply not got enough hours in the day to get through them all,' said Liam. 'He'd do it all if he could, but he's also doing up an old boat over at Bamton Boatyard, and he drives the bus sometimes… and the fish van…'

'And I'm guessing poor old Hattie likes to see him sometimes too?' laughed Lizzie.

'Yeah. That!' said Liam with a grin. 'Luckily, she's just as busy and nutty as he is, so it seems to work out. But I'm more than happy to take on some of the work. I can turn up in the evenings, and some folks seem to really like that if they're at work all day. Hopefully, it'll free Ben up a bit, as well as giving him someone else he can call out in an emergency.'

'Sounds like a great plan,' said Lizzie, feeling awful for dragging him away when he was clearly run off his feet. 'You know, you should have just told me how to get to Ted's place... I could have driven myself!'

'Give over,' laughed Liam. 'I love any excuse to go on an adventure! Besides, Ted's barn is hard to find unless you know where you're going.'

Lizzie nodded. She had to agree with that. Liam had headed out of town and set off towards the Old Schoolhouse to begin with, but then they seemed to have meandered through the lanes in ever-decreasing circles.

'And... why exactly are you taking me to Ted's mysterious barn?' said Lizzie. She'd been trying different variations of this question ever since he'd picked her up, but Liam was yet to give her a straight answer.

'You'll see!' he said with a grin.

'I can't believe I got in a van with a random stranger,' chuckled Lizzie. 'I mean – "heading to Ted's barn" – that's the start of every horror film I've ever heard of!'

'Erm... I'm hardly a random stranger, considering we've known each other since we were kids,' spluttered Liam.

'Well... okay... you do have a point,' said Lizzie. 'I'm

not sure we really *knew* each other back then though. More like... aware of each other?'

'Yeah,' laughed Liam. 'You were way too cool to "know" me. I was a gawky little thing...'

'I can assure you I definitely *wasn't* cool!' said Lizzie indignantly. 'I've never been cool.'

As far as she was concerned, she'd been the weird kid who was happier on her bike than playing with the others. She'd never really cared whether she was on her own or leading a little pack behind her. As long as she had the wind in her hair and was pedalling like a lunatic - that's all she'd ever really cared about.

'I beg to differ,' said Liam. 'You didn't care what you looked like or what anyone thought of you. That's *exactly* what made you so cool!'

'Well... erm... thanks!' said Lizzie.

Liam shrugged. 'I was so desperate to hang out with you. I don't think I ever cycled so far in my life as I did back then, but I loved trying to keep up with you!'

'Well... it's nice to hang out now,' said Lizzie.

'Yup. Sure is,' said Liam.

'So... where exactly are you taking me?' she tried again.

'You're not very patient are you?' he laughed.

'It's not my strong point, no!' said Lizzie.

'We're going to see Ted Hatherleigh,' he said.

Lizzie waited for more of an explanation, but Liam just stopped talking and smiled serenely to himself.

'You told me that already,' she huffed. 'I meant – *why?!* Not that I'm not grateful, of course!'

'You'll see!' said Liam.

Lizzie tutted and crossed her arms. Liam chuckled, clearly not in the least bit bothered. It made a nice change. Mark had never quite been able to tell when she was mucking around and had regularly accused her of being in a mood – which then instantly became a self-fulfilling prophecy.

It really wasn't any wonder their marriage had imploded, was it?! In fact, Lizzie had a sneaking suspicion it would have disintegrated a lot sooner if it hadn't been for the girls. She blinked hard as the van clonked over a bump in the road, bringing her sharply back to the present.

'I hope you don't mind me doing the driving,' said Liam.

'Mind? laughed Lizzie. 'It's great, thanks! Anyway… I'm not entirely sure where my car keys are. I don't think I've seen them since I moved in!'

If she was honest, she was thoroughly enjoying being chauffeured around so that she could stare out of the window at the lanes. She couldn't wait to get out on a bike and explore. Of course – there was only one little hitch with that… she didn't currently own one. It was ironic really, considering she was about to open a bike shop.

Lizzie let out a long sigh.

'You okay?' said Liam, shooting a glance at her. 'Won't be long now!'

'I'm fine,' said Lizzie. 'Just wishing I had my bike with me, that's all.'

'Didn't you bring it down with you?' said Liam in surprise.

'It got nicked before I moved!' she huffed.

'Bummer!' said Liam. 'That's one thing you've got to say for Seabury – at least it's pretty safe.'

'Yeah,' said Lizzie. 'You know - I think that's half the problem. Seabury spoiled me. Even though I lived in the city for over a decade, I never quite got my head around the need to lock everything up. I guess I just wanted it to be like Seabury – safe and friendly.'

'Do you regret leaving?' said Liam with interest.

'Yes and no,' said Lizzie. 'I mean, I've got a feeling the teenage years would have been a bit less white-knuckle down here compared to shepherding two beautiful girls through puberty in a city full of exciting and interesting ways to cause havoc. But... at the time, moving up there was the right thing to do. It was breaking Mark's heart to be away from the girls so much.'

'And being away from you too!' said Liam.

Lizzie shot him a look.

'Sorry!' he said quickly. 'Sorry... I mean... I know you're not together anymore... I just meant back then... sorry...'

Lizzie reached out and patted his arm. 'Breathe!' she

laughed. 'It's absolutely fine. Yeah – I mean, I think we'd already started to drift apart by the time I moved to Bristol - but there was no way I was ready to give up on us. I still thought we could make it work.'

'Wow, sounds really tough,' said Liam with a frown, turning down a lane that was so narrow, it almost felt as though the van was having to hold its breath and suck its belly in.

'Not tough,' said Lizzie, 'just really sad. We stayed together until Jenna left home – she's the youngest – and then, six weeks later, Mark moved out too.'

'What - so soon?' said Liam. 'That's harsh.'

'Not really,' said Lizzie with a shrug. 'It was inevitable by that point. It was a relief for both of us, to be honest. We got together when we were really young – and you do a lot of changing and growing up, don't you? Some people are lucky and grow in the same direction. Not us though. It didn't take long before our only common point was the kids. I think we'll always be close, though. We're just happier divorced than we were married.'

Liam let out a long, slow whistle through his teeth. 'I'm feeling very petty over here. As far as I'm concerned, my ex can go and swim with some eager jellyfish.'

'Ouch!' said Lizzie with a little wince.

'Ouch pretty much sums us up.'

'Sorry,' said Lizzie.

Liam shrugged. 'It is what it is. I married the egotistical, cheating...' He cleared his throat. 'I'm over it by the way. I just enjoy letting off a bit of steam sometimes.'

'Was it recent?' said Lizzie curiously.

'Nope – four... nearly five years now,' said Liam.

'About the same as me then,' said Lizzie.

She glanced at him, wondering if she dared ask if he was still single. No – maybe not. They might be sharing their sob stories, but that would make it sound like she was on the hunt – and she most definitely *wasn't*.

'So...' said Liam as he navigated a tight turn through a gateway that was half-covered with ivy, 'did your ex move on?'

'You'd better believe it!' Lizzie snorted. 'He jumped straight into an affair with one of the secretaries at the office.'

'Eww – cliché, much?' said Liam.

'Yep!' said Lizzie. 'Then, the minute our divorce came through, the pair of them were engaged.'

'Shiiit!' said Liam. 'How are you so calm about it all?'

'Because... I wanted him to be happy?' said Lizzie with a shrug. 'He's a good guy. Mostly. And for some strange reason, Tiff makes him happy.'

'Again - I am feeling very, very small right now,' said Liam, pulling the van to a standstill in front of an immaculate stretch of grass. 'You're still really cool, you know!'

'Am *so* not,' laughed Lizzie. 'Trust me, I've had plenty of time to refine my story and leave out all the snot, tears and swearing that actually went on. I might not have loved Mark anymore, but it still felt like a thump in the chest.'

'Well thank heavens for that,' chuckled Liam. 'At least I know your human! And… are you seeing anyone now?'

'Hold that thought!' said Lizzie, spotting an elderly gent as he appeared around the corner of the huge, modern garage in front of them. He began hobbling towards them, leaning heavily on a stick as he went. 'I'm guessing that's Ted?'

'The one and only,' said Liam with a nod. 'Come on – let's get the pair of you introduced!'

CHAPTER 7

Lizzie clambered down from the van and leaned against the side for a brief moment. She wasn't sure what Ted Hatherleigh might be able to do to help her with her current predicament, but she was intensely grateful that he'd appeared at that exact moment. She'd been enjoying her gossip with Liam, but that last question had made her heart leap into her throat, and she was more than grateful to escape the confines of the van and grab a couple of seconds to pull herself together!

Still... she didn't want Liam to think she was weird, so she forced a smile onto her face and started to make her way around the other side of the van to join him.

Lizzie couldn't help but peer around her as she went. After the overgrown lane and wild hedges, this was all quite a shock. The wide expanse of grass they'd pulled up to was manicured to within an inch of its life

– complete with quintessential bowling-green stripes. The garden surrounding it, however, was completely tangled and wild – full of honeysuckle and crab apple trees.

As for the barn... well, when Liam told her they were going to drive to "Ted's barn", she'd been picturing something quaint and historic – not a modern blockwork garage complete with a roll-up, metal door.

'It's what's inside that counts! Don't let the appearance fool you,' muttered Liam as she came to stand next to him.

'What – do you mean Ted or the garage?' said Lizzie, shooting him a quick wink.

'Oi – I heard that!' said the old man with a barking laugh as he limped towards them across the immaculate grass.

'I'm so sorry!' said Lizzie, horrified.

How on earth had he caught that from all the way over there? The man must have the hearing of a bat!

'One of the perks of these new-fangled hearing aids!' said Ted with a wicked smile. 'That - and turning them off when Margie starts mithering on about something!'

'You know she does that to you too, right?' said Liam with a laugh, hurrying over to Ted to shake his hand.

'Where'd you think I learned the trick?!' said Ted

with a little shake of his walking stick. 'Now then, who's this firecracker?'

'I'm Lizzie,' she said, following Liam's lead and shaking the old man's hand.

'Lizzie Moore!' he said, his eyes twinkling. 'You're just as cheeky as you were when you were little.'

'You remember me?!' said Lizzie.

'Of course – you were a terror on these lanes – always leading a pack of kiddies with you on that snazzy little silver bike of yours!'

'I loved that bike!' said Lizzie with a little sigh. 'I can't remember what happened to it... nan probably gave it away when I got too big!'

'Sounds like your nan!' said Ted. 'Kind to a fault, that woman. I know Margie still misses her.'

'Yeah,' said Lizzie, 'I do too.'

Ted leaned forwards and gave her arm a gentle pat with his free hand. 'She thought you were the bee's knees, that's for certain. What brings you back to Seabury, Lizzie? Visiting?'

'Nope,' said Lizzie. 'I'm back for good.'

'What, to live in your nan's old place again?' said Ted. 'Below the allotments? Like before?'

'Yes. Back in my dream home,' sighed Lizzie. 'But not *quite* like before.'

'Lizzie's opening a bike shop!' said Liam, the words spilling out of him like a shaken can of coke.

Lizzie shot him a grateful smile. She wasn't sure if he was just trying to save her from the tricky subject of her missing husband or if he was just genuinely excited about her shop. Either way, she was glad for an excuse to exit memory lane.

'A bike shop? Are you indeed?' said Ted, his bushy eyebrows shooting up. 'Well then, I think you'd better come with me.'

'Oo...kay?' she said slowly. She turned to Liam with a questioning look, but he just grinned and nodded for her to follow.

What on earth were these two up to?

With a shrug, Lizzie decided to go with the flow. She was here now so she might as well find out what the big surprise was. Besides, she rather liked Ted and that mischievous twinkle in his eye.

'Stupid stick,' muttered Ted, tossing it away so that he could use both hands on the garage door. 'The blasted thing is Margie's idea and I can't stand it.'

Liam ambled forwards to help. 'Lawn's looking good,' he said as the door began to roll upwards

'Thanks!' said Ted. 'That's the *Bryant*. I've finally got it mowing a treat. Took a bit of doing, that did... I had to make a couple of the parts myself – they don't make them like that anymore. Not too many people have the skills anymore!'

If Lizzie was in any doubt as to what the *Bryant* was, they were cleared up the moment she peered inside the garage. There were dozens of ancient lawn-mowers in there, in various states of disrepair.

'Ignore that,' said Ted, nodding to a rather snazzy

sign on the wall that said "The Barn" in swirly gold lettering. 'That's Margie's idea of a joke. I think she wanted to make the place sound grand. Poor old girl, getting stuck with me. She always wanted a big house, and instead, she got stuck with a grubby little cottage and a garage full of lawnmowers!'

'At least she got manicured lawns,' said Liam.

'Aye… poor girl, that she did!' said Ted, his eyes twinkling. 'Anyway, you follow me through here, young Lizzie, and see if you can't win me some brownie points with my wife while you're here.'

Completely at a loss again, Lizzie threw a pleading look at Liam, hoping that he might take pity on her and explain what was going on. Sadly, Liam was too busy admiring one of the ancient mowers to notice.

'Mind your head through here, there's all sorts hanging up to keep them out of the way,' said Ted from somewhere in the gloom in front of her.

Ducking her head and doing her best not to trip over any of Ted's treasures as she went, Lizzie picked her way towards the back of the garage.

'I'll get them all running eventually,' said Ted as she joined him. He patted the handle of yet another mower. 'Or - I will if Margie ever gives me a moment's peace!'

Lizzie smiled. The way Ted spoke about the mythical Margie made her think of her own grandparents – they'd been completely devoted to each other. They'd loved nothing more than to grumble and grouch, but Lizzie had known from an early age that it was a sign of their total love and adoration for each other.

'Right,' said Ted as the pair of them finally reached the back wall, 'bikes, you say?'

Lizzie nodded. 'At least, I hope so. I've hit a bit of a snag with getting all the parts and tools I need... but I'll make it work... somehow...'

'You follow me through here,' said Ted, opening a door in the back wall that Lizzie hadn't even noticed. She followed him through the doorway and then came to a dead stop.

'Wow!' breathed Lizzie.

So this was where bicycles came to retire! This hidden room was almost as large as the first - and it was full of bikes. They were, quite literally, everywhere she looked – hanging from the walls and ceiling, piled in bits in the corners, and standing upside-down in the middle of the room as though Ted was right in the middle of working on them.

Lizzie took in a deep breath and let the scent of metal and oil wash over her. Bikes had a special smell... maybe it was something to do with the tyres, but Lizzie always liked to think that it had something to do with all the adventures they'd been on over the years.

'Hey... wait a minute!' she gasped, moving towards a long workbench that ran along the entire back wall. Above it, hanging from the wall was... 'Isn't that...?'

'Your old bike!' grinned Ted.

Lizzie gaped. The little child's bike was unmissable

– it still had the silver tassels she'd tied to the handlebars and a tiny row of daisy stickers she'd pressed onto each of the peddles. 'How on earth…?'

'Whoever your nan gave it to must have left it in the hedge over near Mrs Scott's place,' said Ted. 'It sat there for about a month and then I thought I'd rescue it and bring it back here. I asked around, but no one claimed it, so it's just been here ever since.'

'And when you say ever since…?' said Lizzie.

'Time doesn't really exist in here,' said Ted with a laugh. 'That's why I like coming out here. Anyway, I expect I've got some other bits of your old bikes around here somewhere. Your nan asked me to take them when she was having a bit of a clear out – before you and your hubby moved in.'

'Ex hubby now, I'm afraid,' said Lizzie, figuring she may as well set him straight before they went any further.

'Ah. Well, I would say I'm sorry, but sometimes it's for the best,' said Ted.

'You're right!' said Lizzie, looking at him in surprise.

'Of course I'm right,' said Ted. 'Your nan always said he was a nice enough chap, but not the right one for you.'

'I know,' sighed Lizzie. 'She wasn't shy about telling me that, either.'

'I can imagine. She was a firecracker - just like you!'

laughed Ted. 'Anyway – speaking of inconvenient spouses…'

'Oof, she'll hear you if you're not careful,' laughed Liam, coming through the door and catching them up at last.

'I don't mind if she does,' said Ted, grinning at him. 'Maybe it'd stop her mithering for a minute!'

'You realise this man adores his wife, right?' said Liam in a fake whisper.

'I got that impression,' laughed Lizzie.

'Too blummin' right I do,' said Ted, suddenly serious. 'That woman is my own personal angel. Just don't tell her I said that, or I'll never hear the last of it. Anyway – that's where you come in, young Lizzie.'

'Sorry, you've lost me!' she said in surprise.

'My old hands aren't what they used to be, and I don't do anything with the bikes anymore, fiddly beggars that they are. I much prefer spending my time on the mowers.'

Lizzie could feel her heart starting to patter, but she didn't dare interrupt.

'On top of that, Margie wants me to clear this place out so that we can get a caravan in here.' He paused and pulled a horrified face, making them both laugh. 'I've been putting her off for years, but I think she's finally worn me down. If any of this lot – the bikes, the parts, most of the tools – would come in handy, then they're yours.'

'What?!' said Lizzie, her voice coming out in a

surprised gasp. She'd been hoping that he might let her nab a couple of spare parts and maybe her childhood bike for old-time's sake, but she hadn't expected him to offer her all of it. 'But... I'm really sorry Ted... I can't pay you... not yet, at least.'

'Don't be daft, girl!' said Ted, shaking his head. 'I've got a problem. I need this lot cleared out before my angel files for divorce – and it sounds like you might just be the solution I've been looking for. Two birds with one stone and all that? Besides, I'd love to see a bike shop open up in town. And if I ever need to borrow back any of the tools, I'll know where to find you, won't I?!'

'Are you sure?' she said, desperately trying to keep a sudden rush of excitement and gratitude under control.

'Sure as I need a cuppa and a sit-down!' chuckled Ted. 'If you can sort out taking it all away, then it's all yours.'

'Wow – I don't know how to thank you!' she said, swallowing down a sudden lump of emotion.

'Don't mention it,' said Ted gruffly. 'Bloody caravans... but anything to keep the wife happy, eh?!'

CHAPTER 8

'Quick!' hissed Lizzie, bouncing up and down in her seat. 'Go go go!'

'What?!' laughed Liam, taking his sweet time to get his seatbelt on before coaxing the old van into life.

'I don't want Ted to change his mind!' said Lizzie, crossing her fingers in her lap and trying not to look like she'd completely lost the plot.

'I don't think you need to worry about that,' said Liam, shooting her a smile. 'Did you see his face? He's just thrilled that you're taking everything and that all his treasures are actually going to be put to good use. I think he was dreading everything ending up at the scrapyard when Margie finally loses patience and empties the place herself!'

Lizzie let out a huge, exaggerated shudder. What a horrible thought!

Liam's van was now crammed to bursting with bike parts, all piled in on top of the broken deckchairs and around his window-washing kit and the mysterious object covered with the tarpaulin. He'd lifted the corner for a brief moment, and Lizzie had caught a glimpse of what looked like the gleaming back end of a vintage motorbike. She'd almost begged for a proper look, but Liam had been too busy wrapping a thick blanket around the whole thing so that it would be protected from the various bits of old bike frame she wanted to take back to The Old Grain Store.

It really had been the most amazing afternoon. With Ted and Liam's help, Lizzie had spent the last few hours picking out the best bits from amongst Ted's treasure hoard – the bits that would mean she could get her workshop open for business in her original timeframe.

Every single pile of "junk" – as Margie had put it when she'd appeared with a tray of tea and biscuits – held a surprise. She'd unearthed tools from her wish list, spare parts in every imaginable size and colour, and even an entire box full of brand-new innertubes.

Lizzie had checked and double-checked with Ted that he really was happy for her to help herself to anything she wanted, and in the end, Ted had brought Margie out again.

'Lizzie wants to know if it's really alright for her to take what she wants?' he'd said with a knowing smirk.

Margie had folded her arms across her chest. 'Well,

let's put it like this. If you don't take it, I'll be sending whatever's left to the tip. So... feel free!'

The idea of all those treasures being thrown away had sent a physical pain through Lizzie, and a fine sheen of cold sweat had appeared on her forehead.

'Don't worry,' Margie had chuckled, taking pity on her. 'Take what you want today and just pile up anything else you want us to keep for you.'

'There's no rush. Just come back whenever you're ready for the rest,' Ted had added.

Margie's parting shot had been a lot less gentle. 'Just remember, I know where to find you. If your stuff is still here when my caravan's due to arrive... then the countdown's on for a final tip-run!'

Lizzie grinned to herself. She'd make sure that she came back for the rest of the treasures before Margie even started to think about tip runs. Even if Liam was too busy to do any more trips, she'd beg, borrow or steal a van so that she could finish the job as soon as possible!

'Well,' said Lizzie with a long, happy sigh as Liam navigated his way back through the narrow, over-grown gateway and onto the winding lanes that would eventually lead them back to Seabury, 'it looks like the dream's well and truly back on track!'

'Brilliant!' said Liam. 'Did you get everything you needed?'

'And then some!' said Lizzie, stroking the fat ring binder that was sitting on her lap. 'Did you know it was

Ted who designed and built that tricycle The Sardine uses for their deliveries?'

'Yep!' Liam nodded. 'Trixie is one of Ted's babies!'

'I know – how amazing!'

'Yeah – I think it was a real blow when his hands got too painful to carry on with that kind of work – he was so good at it! What's in the folder?'

'The original designs for the tricycle... and a bunch of designs for other projects he never got the chance to make before his hands seized up!'

'Wow – what a treasure!' said Liam.

'I know,' said Lizzie. 'I can't believe he let me have it!'

She didn't want to say it out loud yet, but a little seed of an idea had started to sprout while Ted had been leafing through the old, slightly yellowed drawings, explaining parts of the various designs to her as he went. Maybe she could have a go at making them herself. Maybe there were layers to this big dream of hers that she hadn't even started to explore yet.

Lizzie stared at her hands, resting on the folder. They were filthy – coated in oil and grease after sorting through piles of chains, handlebars and old-fashioned bike seats. A sure sign of an afternoon well-spent. She glanced across to where Liam's hands rested lightly on the steering wheel. Sure enough, they were exactly the same. He had nice hands. Strong and purposeful... a bit like him really. A little shiver ran down her spine, and Lizzie shifted slightly in her seat to mask the moment.

Liam had been just as excited as her as he'd helped her to sort through Ted's barn. They'd worked well together - organising the treasure trove that had been decades in the making. Lizzie had to admit that she hadn't met anyone she'd clicked with so easily in a long time... in fact, she couldn't remember ever feeling like this.

Oh crikey – she needed to take control of this before it took on a life of its own. She had a feeling she could be in serious danger if she spent too much time thinking about Liam's strong hands and easy-going company.

The whole dating and relationship thing simply didn't feature in her plans right now... she had too much to do! Sure... the future was full of possibilities, but first things first. Lizzie had a business to get up and running, and a grown-up daughter turning up in the next few days who sounded very much like she needed a bit of TLC. Liam - with his grubby hands, lovely legs and cheeky smile - was just going to have to wait!

'Thank you so much, by the way!' said Lizzie as Liam turned down the lane that would lead them onto the seafront at the North Beach end of town.

'What for?' he said.

'Are you kidding me?' laughed Lizzie. 'For introducing me to Ted, for driving me around when you had way better things to do with your time, for helping me find a way out of impending disaster... for letting me fill your van up with pilfered bike bits...'

'Oh. That!' said Liam, shooting her a smile that made her toes curl. 'Well – I'm glad to help. Though I've got a favour to ask you now!'

'Sure – anything!' said Lizzie. She winced slightly. Jeez, did she really need to sound quite so enthusiastic?!

'Cool. Well... if it's alright with you, can I drop this lot off in the morning instead of doing it now?' he said, pulling an apologetic face. 'It'll mean we'll be less likely to incur the wrath of the traffic warden if I stop by nice and early – so I'll be able to pull up on the pavement right outside. It'll make it a lot easier to unload!'

'Of course!' said Lizzie. 'Blimey – that's hardly a favour!'

For one thing, it had been such a brilliant day, she didn't exactly want to risk it ending with Liam getting a parking ticket. For another – she was absolutely exhausted – but in a good way. Her muscles ached from lifting and carrying and sorting, and she could really do with a long soak in the bath.

'So tomorrow then?' said Liam.

'Perfect,' said Lizzie. 'To be honest, it'll probably save me from myself. If we unloaded it all now, I wouldn't be able to resist getting it all organised and put away... and I'd probably still be at it at midnight!'

'I can just imagine!' said Liam. 'Anyway – thanks for today, it's been a real breath of fresh air.'

'What – hanging out in a mouldy barn full of broken bikes and old lawnmowers?' laughed Lizzie.

'That's the one,' said Liam, slowing down to let Lionel cross the road outside Pebble Street before continuing along West Beach. 'And you don't fool me – you were in seventh heaven, getting all grubby!'

'What can I say – I'm a happy little weirdo!' said Lizzie with a shrug.

'Me and you both,' said Liam, indicating and then pulling to a stop outside the Old Grain Store. 'Right, here we are. I'll be over around half eight tomorrow morning if that's okay?'

'Perfect. Thank you!' said Lizzie, undoing her seatbelt and tucking the folder under her arm as she hopped out of the van. She hurried around the front, not wanting him to drive off before she'd said thank you one last time. She tapped on his window, and he rolled it down, smiling at her.

'Thanks again,' she said, suddenly feeling a little bit shy now that they were face to face.

'No worries,' he said, his eyes twinkling. 'Right, I'd better head off before the locals start tutting at me for stopping on the double yellows!'

'Liam... you are one of the locals!' she laughed.

'Oh yeah!' he grinned. 'Well... so are you.'

Lizzie nodded in delight.

'Right, I'd better head off!' he said, as a car pulled up behind him, clearly waiting for Liam to get out of the way.

Lizzie quickly leaned forwards, ducking in through the open window to kiss his cheek, only for Liam to turn back to her just at the wrong moment.

Their lips met with a bump.

'Wow!' said Liam, his eyes wide as he pulled back to stare at her in surprise.

'Sorry!' gasped Lizzie, taking a quick step backwards. 'I was aiming for your cheek!'

'We'll talk about that tomorrow!' said Liam, starting to laugh.

'But-' gasped Lizzie.

She was too late. An irritable *honk* sounded from the car behind, and Liam set off, clearly not wanting to incur the wrath of anyone on the narrow seafront road.

Lizzie quickly scarpered to the safety of the pavement and raised her hand to wave. She couldn't help the huge grin that spread across her face as a grubby, oily hand appeared from Liam's window, waving back as he disappeared up the road.

CHAPTER 9

*I*n a daze, Lizzie turned to stare at The Old Grain Store. She was still clutching Ted's priceless folder to her heart as though it was some kind of comfort blanket that might soothe the mad fluttering that was going on inside her chest.

Why was she such an idiot? Just a nice, normal goodbye would have done the trick. A little wave. A smile. They'd had plenty of chat and banter on the way back to town… and then she'd gone and spoiled it all.

'Get a grip!' she muttered to herself, admiring the lovely clean windows before searching for the keys in the depths of her pockets. She just wanted to pop the folder somewhere safe and sound, close the shutters and then she was planning on treating herself to an early night.

Two minutes later, after a short-lived battle with the shutters that were still decidedly stiff, Lizzie had locked up and was back out on the pavement. She eyeballed the front of her building with a critical eye. It wouldn't take too much more work to get ready for her grand opening. A lick of paint... a bit of work on the shutters... and a name.

Lizzie had been struggling with what to call her new shop for ages – after all, she couldn't just keep calling it the Old Grain Store, could she? It didn't exactly scream "bicycle shop!" Ah well - something would come to her eventually – she was sure of it! After somehow managing to dodge almost-certain disaster, figuring out a name suddenly felt like child's play by comparison.

Now that she knew her own big dream was still on, Lizzie needed to turn her thoughts to welcoming Jenna to the cottage. She'd need to move some boxes around so that she could find somewhere for her to sleep – but she quickly reminded herself that her youngest was used to living in the back of a van, so it wasn't like she was going to be too picky, was it?!

'Right... home time!' Lizzie muttered, crossing the road and staring out to sea for a moment. She loved the view from this end of West Beach back towards the centre of town. From here she could see the King's Nose jutting out into the sea behind the Pebble Street Hotel. Beyond that, high on the far point, stood the lighthouse where, according to Ethel, Seabury's two loved-up café owners now lived.

Lizzie let out a long sigh. Maybe she'd end up being

friends with Kate… and Lou… she certainly hoped so. It had been wonderful spending time with Liam today simply because they seemed to be on the same wavelength. With any luck, she'd find plenty more people like that here too. If there was one thing she wanted, now that she was back, it was to fill her life with special people… because what else could be better than cramming every single day with as much friendship as she could get her hands on?!

As she started to climb the hill back towards the cottage, Lizzie couldn't help but run through the list of jobs she still had to do. Hopefully, she'd manage to get a second wind this evening so that she could clear enough space for Jenna. Then, perhaps she could head back down to the shop early tomorrow morning and get some painting done before Liam arrived with his van…

Lizzie's heart started to race as she wondered what Liam was like with a paintbrush. Suddenly her head was filled with the image of him with a pair of overalls tied around his waist and splatters of paint in his hair.

'Blimey!' puffed Lizzie, struggling to catch her breath. It was just the hill… and those flutterings were just because she was ravenous. After all, she hadn't eaten anything since that pastry Liam had brought her. She just needed some food… and to get her mind onto a safer topic!

The minute Lizzie reached the cottage, she let herself in and marched straight through to the kitchen, intent on finding something to eat in the vague hope that it might help her feel a bit more grounded and stop all this floaty nonsense she had going on in her head.

Hmm... not exactly inspiring!

That was the problem with being so busy and getting caught up with her plans and worries... she was completely losing track of the basics – like food shopping! She'd definitely need to rectify that before Jenna arrived.

For now, she'd just have to make do because she certainly didn't have the energy to hunt for her car keys and head out to buy groceries after the day she'd had!

After ten minutes of rooting around in the cupboards and the large cardboard box on the kitchen table marked "store cupboard", Lizzie started to throw together a quick meal. She piled up crackers, pickles and olives, along with the last remaining chunk of cheddar from the fridge, and one of the apples that had travelled down with her on the move. Lizzie quickly cut it in quarters and took a test bite. Not the best – but at least it hadn't quite turned into a tasteless potato yet.

Lizzie added the apple to the plate and stared down at her tea. Well... it certainly wouldn't win any awards for presentation - but at least it would fill a hole. She had to admit, she was looking forward to trying out the food at the Pebble Street Hotel. Ted had been telling her about it earlier, and even Margie had waxed lyrical on the subject. According to her, Hattie's cooking was nothing short of sublime – especially her puddings.

Carrying her plate through to the living room, Lizzie let out a huge groan when she spotted that the sofa had a mini mountain of fresh washing heaped at one end, and there were a couple of boxes piled precariously on the other end.

'Damnit!' she muttered.

Balancing the plate on the top box, Lizzie gathered the washing together in one giant, unruly armful, and proceeded to turn in a circle looking for somewhere else to put it. The loud, impatient growl from her stomach brought things to a head, and she marched out into the hallway and dumped the entire lot unceremoniously onto the floor at the bottom of the stairs. She'd sort it out later!

Stomping back through to the living room, Lizzie lowered herself carefully onto the sofa next to the boxes and grabbed her plate. She'd just managed to gather a bit of everything onto the corner of a cracker when her mobile phone begin to vibrate in her back pocket, making her jump. The laden cracker crumbled back onto the plate, and she sighed.

Ah well... small mercies... at least it hadn't landed on the floor!

Plonking the plate back on top of the box, Lizzie shifted her weight and yanked her mobile out of her pocket.

'Megan?' she said in surprise.

It was rare her eldest daughter ever called her – it was usually the other way around. Even rarer than that were the squeaking, sniffling sounds issuing coming from the phone.

'Meggie?' she said again, reverting to her pet name for her little girl, 'what's the matter lovely?'

Megan instantly started to jabber so fast that Lizzie had a hard time trying to figure out what she was saying. The reception in the cottage wasn't the best... but it definitely wasn't helped by the copious amounts of snotty tears going on at Megan's end.

'Slow down, Meggie,' she said gently, her heart hammering as worry mounted in her chest. What on earth could have got her steady, driven, focused daughter in such a tizz? 'Tell me what's wrong.'

'Focus mother!' blubbed Megan. 'I didn't get the promotion and I think Owen just split up with me!'

'Oh!' said Lizzie, secretly thinking that being rid of the most boring man in the world wasn't something to get upset about. And hadn't Megan been promoted just a matter of weeks ago?

'It's all such a mess,' she sobbed.

Lizzie was alarmed to hear her voice quivering again.

'What can I do, Meggie?' she said gently.

'I need to get out of here!' said Megan, sounding urgent now. 'Upstairs have got the builders in, they're renovating their flat. I mean – how am I supposed to concentrate and get my life back on track with that racket going on? Owen was meant to propose, mum – it's on my planner!'

Lizzie shook her head, feeling slightly dazed as Megan started off with another round of sobbing.

'When?' she said. 'Why?'

'It was part of my pl-a-a-n!' blubbed Megan. 'Now it's ruined and I've got to get back on tra-a-ack!'

Lizzie bit her lip, fighting down the horrifying urge to laugh. Maybe this was why the girls usually turned to their dad for support?! Before she could pull herself together and manage to get a word in edgeways, Megan was off again.

'I need a couple of weeks away from it all, mum – otherwise I don't know *what* I'm going to do!'

'Don't say things like that!' said Lizzie, horrified.

'I mean it! I might... I might... end up like Jenna!' she said, as though this was the worst thing she could possibly imagine.

This time, Lizzie couldn't help but let out a laugh.

'It's not funny,' huffed Megan. 'I'm serious! I'm coming down to stay with you for a couple of weeks. I tried calling dad and I can't get through so it's going to have to be Seabury. I'll be there the day after tomorrow.'

Lizzie did her best to fight down the customary stab of hurt that - once again – she'd been the backup parental choice and that Megan, like Jenna, had turned to Mark first. She opened her mouth to warn Megan that her sister was also descending on Seabury in the next few days, but she was too late – Megan had already disappeared.

'Oh for goodness sake!' tutted Lizzie.

She wasn't sure whether to laugh or to cry, so instead she grabbed her plate. Staring at the crummy, less-than-appetising mess, she promptly changed her mind. It was time to dig out the emergency bar of chocolate.

CHAPTER 10

Lizzie yawned widely as she rinsed out the dregs of her morning coffee and set the mug down on the draining board. She scrubbed at her eyes with her still-damp hands. They felt gritty, and she had a sneaking suspicion that she had eyebags the size of suitcases - not that she'd know, of course, because she hadn't had a moment to glance in the mirror yet.

It had been another night that had included very little sleep. Lizzie's brain had insisted on running through her to-do list on a loop – it had grown substantially longer following Megan's phone call. The fact that darkness had also been punctuated by unsettling flashbacks of her accidental lip-bash with Liam definitely hadn't added a sense of calm to the situation!

In the end, she'd given up on sleep and had hauled herself out of bed early to see what she could do about moving enough cardboard boxes out of the way so that the girls would have somewhere to stay when they descended. Lizzie thought she might just about be able to clear one of the spare rooms in time, but there was no way she'd be able to sort the second one out. There were simply too many boxes – piled high from floor to ceiling.

There was plenty of room outside the front of the cottage of course, and Lizzie had briefly considered stashing some of the boxes under a tarpaulin... but she'd given up on that idea pretty quickly. She simply didn't have the energy to lug all her worldly possessions back down the stairs. Besides – what if it rained?

Her next bright idea had been to shift some of the boxes down to The Old Grain Store, but that would mean delaying opening the shop – and after risking the entire plan when she'd bailed Jenna out, she wasn't willing to do it again by turning the space into a dumping ground!

Lizzie had even considered calling Mark and asking for his help. Both the girls had mentioned they'd tried to reach out to their dad before calling her – and as much as that hurt - right now she could actually do with him pulling one of his "super-dad" moments. If they could just stay with him for the first week to give her a tiny bit longer to get herself sorted out, it would be a huge help.

Lizzie had bided her time, waiting until it was a more socially acceptable hour to call her ex and ask for a favour… but when the time came, she'd changed her mind. Even though she was still on excellent terms with Mark, the same couldn't be said for his new wife. The possibility of getting Tiffany on the phone at any time of day was enough to make Lizzie shudder in horror, and the thought of having to speak to her before she'd had the chance to sink a second coffee was simply inconceivable.

'Come on Lizzie!' she huffed, leaning heavily against the sink. There *had* to be a way to fit three adults into a house with three decent-sized bedrooms! If only her worldly goods weren't taking up every last inch of space, it would have been an absolute doddle. Instead, it was just a complete nightmare.

There wasn't time to organise it all, but she couldn't just abandon the girls. She *was* their mum after all – even if the pair of them were more than old enough to fend for themselves.

Urgh! She was officially too tired to deal with this right now!

Lizzie glanced at the kitchen clock and swore. She had precisely three minutes before she was meant to be down at the shop to help Liam unload the van!

∼

'Morning, bright eyes!'

Lizzie smiled wearily as she approached the van, and Liam climbed out to greet her. As promised, he'd pulled it right up onto the pavement outside the shop... though goodness knows how long he'd been waiting for her to turn up.

'I'm so sorry I'm late!' she said, puffing as she tried to catch her breath from her route-march from the cottage. At least it was all downhill – but that's about all that could be said in its favour this morning. She'd have brought the car... but she still hadn't managed to unearth the keys.

'You okay?' said Liam, raising his eyebrows in mild concern as he made his way around the back of the van to open the doors.

'Yeah – yeah fine!' said Lizzie, nodding. She suddenly felt a bit shy as she remembered their awkward bump-kiss from the day before. 'Erm... you've not been waiting too long, have you?' she said, fumbling in her cardigan pocket and praying that she hadn't managed to forget the keys to The Old Grain Store in her mad rush to get down here.

'Nah – don't worry about that!' said Liam. 'Though, I do need to get a bit of a wiggle on. Lionel gave me the heads up that a bunch of new visitors have just arrived at the hotel. It's not a bad day, so you never know - they might fancy a deckchair and a good lounge around on West Beach. I want to be ready to pounce!'

Lizzie smiled. She quickly dismissed the idea of asking Liam if he fancied joining her for breakfast in The Sardine when they were finished. She'd have loved nothing more than a bacon roll... and the chance to talk to him about a couple of things. Mostly, she wanted to apologise properly for that awkward kiss... but she also wanted to ask him for his advice about her daughter predicament!

Lizzie was glad to be back in Seabury – but she had to admit she was missing her friends back in Bristol this morning. She needed someone she could offload to – someone who knew her well enough that she could have a damn good whinge without the risk of any kind of judgement.

Ah well... maybe it was a good thing Liam was busy after all! To be fair to the poor guy, he'd already done *more* than his fair share of Lizzie-sitting for one week!

The pair of them worked in near-silence as they ferried box after box of bike bits into the shop in a kind of relay – one of them keeping an eye out for the parking warden while the other nipped inside.

The last piece to come out of the van was Lizzie's little silver bike – and just the sight of it brought a smile to her face. She might not know what her new shop was going to be called yet – but she knew exactly what the centrepiece of her first window display was going to be!

'Right – that's you all sorted,' said Liam, closing the van doors with a *thunk*. 'Have fun sorting it all out – and just let me know when you want to go and collect some more!'

'Oh I couldn't possibly ask you to-'

'Of course you can!' said Liam firmly. 'Right – I'd better be off!'

Before she even had the chance to thank him properly, Liam had hopped up into the driver's and was on his way.

Blimey... he really *was* desperate to get his deckchairs set up! Either that or Liam was scared she was going to attempt a repeat performance of yesterday's kiss!

'Oh shut up!' Lizzie huffed at herself crossly. The poor guy was just busy.

She turned and marched herself back inside, determined to get as much work done as humanly possible before tiredness forced her to go on the hunt for more coffee.

Closing the door carefully behind her so that she wouldn't be disturbed, Lizzie got to work, sorting through the goodies they'd just unloaded and arranging them on the shelves of her workshop area. She'd been looking forward to this, but she was so distracted that she worked on autopilot, her head full to bursting as she tried to figure out the logistics of having both the girls to stay at the same time.

Maybe she could just ask Jenna and Megan to share a room...

'Yeah right!' she muttered with a snort as she coiled a loose bike chain.

They'd given that a go when they'd first moved to Bristol and it had been an unmitigated disaster! It had lasted all of two weeks before they'd become so sick of the constant arguing that Mark had given up his home office so that Jenna could use it as her bedroom.

Of course, the girls were both in their twenties now, and - in theory – were grown-ups. But Lizzie had moved to Seabury for a quiet life, and she had a feeling that making them share a room would result in the exact opposite.

Perhaps she should just give up her own bedroom for a while? She could sleep in the living room, couldn't she? After all, Lizzie didn't care if there were cardboard boxes stacked up in the corners. That wouldn't work either, though, because Jenna was a complete night owl. She loved to stay up late, burning incense and listening to Joni Mitchel on repeat. She never got to bed much before two in the morning… and there was no way Lizzie could exist on so little sleep.

There was always the hotel…

Now there was a thought! Lizzie could just leave the girls to fight it out between them and treat herself to a room at Pebble Street. Liam had said that there were a bunch of new visitors there, but the place was huge. Maybe Lionel still had a room available… it would have to be a really cheap room though, considering her bank account was already running on fumes!

Lizzie closed her tired eyes for a moment and allowed herself to daydream about a lovely hotel room where she could float around in a big, fluffy robe. Just imagine having a restaurant downstairs whenever she fancied something tasty - rather than having to raid her cupboards for increasingly stale crackers! Of course, Pebble Street was just down the road from the shop too... that would be an added bonus!

Lizzie opened her eyes and let the cold light of day pull her out of her delicious daydream. As much as it sounded like heaven to her right now, the girls both needed her. She couldn't just flake out and abandon them for a spot of luxury – no matter how tempting it was.

'Time for a spot of mum duty!' she sighed, running her hands through her hair. She only hoped they'd realise that she'd only just arrived in town herself and that she was still finding her feet.

Maybe they'd lend a hand when they realised how much she had on her plate with getting this place sorted out! They'd be understanding... wouldn't they? They'd see she was busy trying to build a business...

'Yeah, right!' laughed Lizzie, rolling her eyes.

No matter how grown-up her girls thought they were – Lizzie knew that she would always just be "mum" to them.

CHAPTER 11

About an hour into her sorting mission, Lizzie realised that she was wandering around The Old Grain Store in circles carrying the same box, while her thoughts did the same thing – swirling around her worries about the girls in ever-decreasing circles.

It was definitely time for a break! Lizzie promptly plonked the box down right in the middle of the floor and grabbed her bag. Coffee and a quick change of scene should do the trick and help her to get her head on straight again. At the very least the caffeine buzz should give her a bit of energy to get something useful done!

Locking the door behind her, Lizzie strode along the seafront, taking long, deep breaths. The weather was still a bit grumpy out here this morning, and she had a feeling Liam might have been a bit over-optimistic if he was expecting Lionel's new visitors to want to sit around on the beach for long. Sure, it had stopped raining, but there was a stiff wind whipping up from the sea. Tiny swirls of sand kept rising from West Beach and dancing along the surface.

Lizzie peered along the beach, keeping her eyes half closed against the stinging wind. Sure enough, Liam had set up his beautiful chairs on the stretch of sand below The Sardine. As far as she could see from here, only one of them was occupied, and it looked very much like that person was fast asleep, wrapped up in a huge coat despite the fact that it was the middle of summer.

If only she didn't have quite so much to do. Lizzie wouldn't mind a little doze on the beach herself. It would be even better if Liam joined her to keep her warm!

'Stop it!' she muttered. What was *wrong* with her this morning?!

Lizzie could feel a hot blush stinging her cheeks as she spotted Liam pottering up to the deckchairs. She needed to pull herself together.

Shaking her head as though it might help dislodge her troublesome thoughts, Lizzie crossed the little seafront road so that she was as far away from the beach as possible. It was all the distance she could put between herself and Liam right now... but maybe it would help!

What with the wind and her unsettled thoughts – Lizzie felt thoroughly stirred up both on the inside *and* the outside, so she was super-glad when she reached The Sardine. She gave the door a gentle push, but it didn't budge.

Huh! The sign said "Open"...

Lizzie cupped her hands against the glass so that she could see inside, only to catch sight of Ethel's laughing face behind the counter. She seemed to be pointing to the spot just inside the door.

Looking down, Lizzie saw what the problem was immediately. There was a giant, fluffy roadblock lying just inside the door. She watched in amusement as Ethel came out from behind the counter, bent down and patted her knee with one hand, waving what looked like a Rich Tea biscuit with the other.

The fluffy roadblock heaved itself to its feet, and Lizzie watched as the huge Bernese Mountain dog mooched over towards Ethel, its feathery tail wagging as it went. The proffered biscuit disappeared with one, eager chomp.

'I'm guessing that must be Stanley?' laughed Lizzie, taking the opportunity to push the door open while he was otherwise engaged.

'The one and only!' laughed Ethel, tickling the big dog's ears as he stared up at her adoringly. 'Sorry about that – he knows Sarah's due at any moment with some fresh cake. It's like he's got a sixth sense for it, and he likes to lie in wait for her because he knows he'll get the crumbs when she empties the boxes!'

Lizzie smiled down at Stanley as he turned his big

head towards her, panting lazily and swishing his tail slowly from side to side. She'd realised now that she'd seen him once before. She was sure she'd spotted his head sticking out of the sea, paddling for all he was worth directly away from the shore… and a pretty teenage girl had been hollering after him for all she was worth. At the time, Lizzie hadn't been entirely sure he was a dog or a seal!

'Erm, does Stanley like a swim by any chance?' said Lizzie.

'Ha! I'm not sure the word "like" covers it. It drives Kate to distraction because he loves heading out in search of seals to play with,' said Ethel, moving back behind the counter and washing her hands. 'She's had to call Ben to help her out so many times – he's got a little boat you see!'

'You monkey,' said Lizzie, holding out her hand for Stanley to sniff. He promptly leaned his entire head into her palm, demanding tickles.

'What can I get you?' said Ethel.

'Latte please,' said Lizzie, 'to have in, this time.'

'No problem,' said Ethel turning towards the gleaming vintage coffee machine. 'So… it's going to be a bike shop, is it?!'

Lizzie gaped at Ethel, wondering if she'd just heard that right over the whirring of the coffee beans being freshly ground… but given the twinkly look of curiosity Ethel was sending her over her shoulder, she didn't think she'd been mistaken.

Lizzie sighed. Liam must have said something… and she had to admit, she wasn't entirely sure how she felt about that! It wasn't as though she'd sworn him to secrecy or anything, but still…

'Now, don't you go blaming Liam,' said Ethel quickly, showcasing her usual knack for mindreading as she spooned fine coffee grounds into a huge metal puck before tamping it down efficiently. 'We had Margie Hatherleigh in here earlier, and she was all excited because you cleared out so much of Ted's barn yesterday.'

Lizzie opened her mouth to say something but shut it again. She wasn't really sure *what* to say if she was honest. It didn't *really* matter that the news was out… did it? It would have just been nice to at least have a name for her new shop before the whole town knew about it!

'I know you've been away for a good while, Lizzie love,' said Ethel kindly, 'but don't forget that news travels fast around Seabury!'

'You're right there!' Lizzie laughed, nodding. 'I was just thinking I wished that I had a name for the place sorted out. I've been struggling with what to call it.'

Ethel cocked her head for a moment. 'You're using your maiden name again now, aren't you?'

Lizzie nodded.

'Well, that's easy then,' said Ethel. 'How about Moore Bikes?'

'Ethel… you're a genius!' said Lizzie.

'So I've been told,' said Ethel with a grin, popping a perfect latte on the counter.

Lizzie jumped to her feet to grab it, only to hear a mad, drumming sound coming from behind her. She turned around to discover that it was Stanley's tail thumping against the floorboards as he stared avidly at the café door.

Through the glass, Lizzie spotted a young girl balancing a bunch of cake boxes in front of her. She hurried over to open the door.

'Cheers!' said the girl, throwing a grateful smile at Lizzie as she ambled in. She was obviously an expert at keeping her balance while managing to avoid treading on Stanley's paws, because he was now dancing around her in excitement. 'Down!' she said, and Stanley promptly sat on Lizzie's feet.

'So, you must be Lizzie?' said the girl, plonking the boxes down on the nearest table and then turning to smile at her. 'Are you here trying to sell Ethel a Penny Farthing?'

Lizzie snorted in amusement. Wow – the news was *really* spreading fast!

'Young people these days,' huffed Ethel. 'So cheeky!'

'You'd better believe it!' said the girl, giving Ethel a kiss on the cheek and earning herself a one-armed squeeze. 'I'm Sarah, by the way,' she added, grinning at Lizzie.

'Sarah's Mike Pendleton's daughter – Mike owns New York Froth,' said Ethel.

A QUIET LIFE IN SEABURY

'Oh!' said Lizzie, beginning to fit the pieces of the puzzle together. 'So you live up at the lighthouse with your dad and Kate?'

'That's me!' said Sarah. 'But those two are off gallivanting around Italy at the moment. Dad decided Kate deserved a break... though he had a right job getting her to leave Seabury - even for five minutes!'

'I'm not sure if it was Seabury or Stanley she was more reluctant to leave behind,' laughed Ethel.

'It's only for a couple of weeks!' said Sarah with a shrug, ruffling Stanley's fur. 'And she knew we'd look after this idiot! Anyway - I know who you are of course – Lou told us! Your new shop sounds exciting!'

'Erm... thanks!' said Lizzie, getting caught up in the girl's infectious blast of energy.

It *was* exciting! She'd just allowed herself to get caught up in all the stressy nonsense and lost sight of the fact that this was her dream.

'So what have you got for us today?' said Ethel. 'The Chilly Dippers will be in any moment-'

'Chilly Dippers?' said Lizzie.

'Mad bunch of cold water swimmers,' said Sarah. 'Lou goes out with them. Total nutcases, the lot of them... and they always need a good sugar fix afterwards!'

'Oh!' said Lizzie with a shudder at the thought of sea swimming when it was so windy outside.

'Right,' said Sarah, turning back to the boxes. 'I've got toffee apple cake, classic red velvet, fudge-butter scrumdiddlyumptious, and a Deep, Dark and Interesting!'

Lizzie felt her eyes grow wide as Sarah whipped the top off of each of the boxes as she went, revealing one perfect cake after another. The toffee apple cake boasted a shiny, red toffee glaze, the red velvet had perfectly piped poppies coating every last inch of it, and the fudgy-thingummy looked like it would just melt in your mouth.

'What's the deep and dark one?' asked Lizzie, eyeballing the pure-white cake that looked like it had been dusted with charcoal.

'That's one of her newest creations,' said Ethel. 'Folks can't get enough of it.'

'Of course they can't!' said Sarah. 'Bitter chocolate, espresso... with a hint of mystery.'

'What's the mystery?' said Lizzie.

'Ha – good luck with that one!' said Ethel.

'Magic!' said Sarah, wiggling her eyebrows. 'Wait... unless you have any allergies?'

Lizzie shook her head. 'Nope.'

'In that case... magic!' Sarah said again with a laugh. 'So... which one are you going to try?'

'Oh... erm...'

Lizzie hadn't been planning on adding cake to her morning indulgence, but the sweet scent of fresh cake had set her stomach rumbling. Of *course* she was going to have a piece of cake... but how on earth was she going to be able to choose between them!

She watched as Sarah carefully transferred each of the ginormous cakes from their boxes onto the empty stands on the counter, doing her best not to dribble – and still none the wiser.

'How about you have a little bit of each of them?' said Ethel, coming to her rescue with a knowing smirk.

Lizzie was about to come over all polite and protest that *no, she couldn't possibly*, but instead she found herself nodding eagerly.

'Oooh yes please... I can't resist!'

'See, that's music to my ears!' laughed Sarah. 'Do you reckon I can borrow you... you can come into college, sit behind the examiners and whisper nice things like that in their ears!'

'I'll do anything for cake!' laughed Lizzie.

'Sounds like we have a deal!' said Sarah.

'Sarah, love - can I just say you're not going to need any kind of favours to blow those examiners away,' said Ethel, carefully cutting thin slices of each of the magnificent cakes and arranging them on an embarrassingly large dinner plate. 'You know your stuff, young lady! You've had so much hands-on experience, you could probably teach them a thing or two by this point! I mean, look at this glaze – I could use it as a mirror!'

Sarah grinned and tried to wave away the compliment, but Lizzie could see that she was thrilled.

'Here we go!' said Ethel, placing the huge plate full of cake in front of Lizzie.

She picked up a fork and, after a long moment of deliberation, tried a piece of the toffee apple cake with its crisp glaze first.

'Oh my... YUM!' she mumbled, trying not to spray cake crumbs everywhere.

'My point exactly!' said Ethel with an approving nod. 'Our Sarah's going to be famous.'

'I'd have to agree with that!' said Lizzie, scooping up a bit of the fudge cake next.

It was such a shame that neither Megan nor Jenna had any interest in cooking. She had a feeling if they could bake like this, she'd happily shift boxes out of the way until the cows came home. Sadly, the pair of them took after her when it came to cooking... and she could just about use a tin opener.

She wasn't sure if it was the sugar hit or the lovely company that was working its magic, but Lizzie felt like all her worries were fading away as sat in the little café, working her way through her plateful of cake. She'd just made a start on her second coffee when Lizzie became aware that someone was trying to catch her attention.

Looking down towards her feet, she came face to face with Stanley. His big, brown eyes held hers as he stared at her intently. He licked his lips. He didn't blink. It was pretty clear he was waiting for *his* piece of cake from her treat plate.

Lizzie smirked and glanced at her plate to choose a morsel for her new friend. She'd been circling around, taking a bite out of each slice in turn, so there were still three tiny pieces remaining. Hmm... maybe she'd just give him a tiny bit of her least favourite... but no – that was impossible. They were all amazing – completely dribble-worthy in fact. There was nothing for it – she'd just have to close her eyes and pick one.

Her fork landed on the red velvet cake, and she stuck out her bottom lip. But a deal was a deal! Lizzie picked it up and dropped it next to Stanley.

It really was a case of *blink and you'll miss it!* The dog's head dashed down and the cake was gone in a split-second. After a quick polish of the floorboards with his big, pink tongue, Stanley flopped down right across her feet. He was surprisingly heavy – but there was something incredibly comforting about his warmth, even though she could feel the blood being squeezed out of her toes.

'Now you've done it!' laughed Ethel. 'Looks like you've got a friend for life!'

CHAPTER 12

By the time Lizzie stepped out of The Sardine, she was riding high on far too much cake and coffee. She felt about one thousand percent better… and now she couldn't really get her head around what all the fuss had been about.

If she didn't know better, Lizzie would bet anything that Sarah had spiked the Deep, Dark and Interesting cake with something decidedly dodgy – but she felt pretty confident that there was no way the straight-talking Ethel would let anything like that happen under her watch!

The wind seemed to have become even stronger while she'd been busy loading up with sugar and caffeine, and Lizzie paused to pull on her cardigan. She was almost done when a group of decidedly damp women appeared from the direction of the beach.

The Chilly Dippers swirled around Lizzie, clearly

intent on warming up inside The Sardine. They were wrapped up in everything from oversized jumpers to towels with wellington boots sticking out underneath.

Suddenly, she realised that one of them was waving in her direction. Lizzie turned and peered over her shoulder, assuming there must be someone behind her – but the pavement was empty. She turned back to the woman - who was wearing a brilliantly mad swimming cap with dozens of bright plastic flowers stuck all over it – and smiled at her tentatively.

'I'm L... L... Lou,' she stuttered as she reached Lizzie. Her lips looked slightly blue. 'L... L... Loved your house. C... C... Catch up soon when I've got more c... c... clothes on?'

'I'd love that!' said Lizzie, thrilled to finally meet her old lodger. 'You know where to find me!'

Lou gave her a juddering nod. 'C... c... cottage or b... b... bike shop!' She forced a smile onto her shivering lips and gave Lizzie the thumbs up - almost dropping her towel in the process.

'Go! Warm up!' said Lizzie, ushering her in the direction of The Sardine and then shaking her head in amusement as the rest of the group rushed past her and piled into the tiny café behind Lou. Something told her Sarah's delicious cakes stood no chance of survival against that lot!

Well – if Lou knew about the bike shop too, it looked like the news was well and truly out. Lizzie tilted her head for a moment, testing out how she really felt about her secret travelling around the Seabury grapevine at warp speed. She promptly came to the conclusion that she didn't mind in the slightest. In fact, she was rather impressed. It wasn't even ten in the morning and she'd only visited the Hatherleigh's barn yesterday!

Well, at least it boded well for when she wanted to do a bit of marketing – maybe she should see if Margie wanted a bit of work! Thank heavens Ethel had given her the heads up that it was Margie who'd let the cat out of the bag – at least it would save her from making an idiot out of herself by accusing Liam of saying something.

Thinking about Liam made her want to say hello again, and now that she had all that sugar coursing through her system she was feeling a lot braver about it than earlier. Maybe she'd just stop by briefly on her way back to The Old Grain Store. After all, she needed to carry on with her mammoth task of sorting all those goodies out so that she'd be ready to fetch the next load from Ted's barn as soon as possible.

Lizzie crossed the road and ran lightly down the steps onto the sandy beach. Well – there were the chairs... or at least *most* of the chairs! It looked like a gust of wind had got hold of one of them and was busy whisking it along the beach, with Liam hot on its heels.

Huh – maybe now wasn't the best time after all!

Liam hesitated, clearly catching sight of her, but with a quick wave, he continued the chase. For a brief moment, Lizzie wondered if she should join in – but promptly decided against it. Her feet hadn't quite regained full circulation after playing dog-bed for Stanley for the past half an hour... and besides, she'd never been much of a runner anyway.

Lizzie was watching Liam pelt along the sand, trying not to be too blatant about the fact that she was admiring his bum, when one of the deckchairs nearest her collapsed, making her jump out of her skin. She spun around to stare at it.

The wind was whipping the canvas of the empty chairs into a frenzy, and she hurried over to put a hand on one just as it tried to lurch off down the beach and follow its friend towards the sea. Somehow, she doubted Liam was going to get many customers today – the sky might be blue, but there was a good chance this little lot were going to take off at any moment.

'Hey!' Liam called in greeting as soon he was back within shouting distance. The wayward deckchair was now neatly folded and tucked under his arm – though it seemed to be acting a bit like a sail. Every couple of steps, Liam stumbled sideways as the canvas billowed and threatened to pull him off his feet.

'Hi!' said Lizzie, grinning over at him. 'Erm – that chair fainted and this one seems to want to go for a wander too!' she laughed, taking a slightly firmer hold on the wooden frame and wincing slightly as one of the others decided to fold in on itself.

'Yep – time to give it up as a bad job for the day,'

said Liam, tossing his burden onto the sand and quickly moving to dismantle the front row of chairs before any of them could make a break for it.

Without thinking about it, Lizzie started to do the same with the back row. 'Where do they need to go?' she said, raising her voice slightly as the wind roared past her ears.

Liam pointed to a little cabin near the pavement. It was a little garden shed that had been decorated to resemble a tiny beach hut. It had been beautifully painted and firmly strapped down to several heavy concrete blocks – clearly a precaution against it ending up in the sea.

Lizzie quickly gathered a couple of the chairs together and hauled them towards the hut with her head bowed in an attempt not to get a mouthful of swirling sand while she was at it.

The minute she stepped inside the shed, she let out a sigh. Just to be out of the wind for a second was a huge relief.

'Blimey!' laughed Liam as he joined her, squeezing into the cramped space. 'That's a bit much for July in Devon! I wouldn't be surprised if we're in for a storm later at this rate.'

'You might be right!' said Lizzie, pushing back her hair and removing several strands from her eyes and mouth before smiling at him. 'Hi, by the way!'

'Hello!' said Liam, smiling at her broadly. 'And thank you!'

'Are you kidding me?' snorted Lizzie. 'I think I owe you so many favours before we're anywhere near even that this one barely even counts!'

'Nah,' said Liam with a shrug. 'It doesn't work like that!'

'I like it in here,' said Lizzie, peering around just to give herself something other than his beautiful smile and lovely crinkly eyes to stare at.

'Yeah – I was lucky that the council agreed for me to have it down here in the summer,' he said. 'They're happy as long as it's off the beach before the end of September.'

'Fair enough,' said Lizzie. 'I mean, that'll be a bit of a pain but...'

Liam shrugged. 'Sean who built it for me said he's happy to stash it at his place over winter, and he'll do any repairs it needs before next year while it's there too.'

'That's brilliant!' said Lizzie. 'Actually... it's given me an idea.'

'Oh yeah?' said Liam.

Lizzie nodded, doing her best to ignore the fact that his eyes seemed to be twinkling at her.

'I don't think I mentioned it earlier – but I've now got both girls descending on me in the next few days,' she said. 'Problem is, I'm up to my eyeballs with moving boxes, and I haven't got time to finish unpacking before they turn up and shifting them all somewhere else would be a nightmare.'

'Especially when you want to be sorting the shop ready to open!' said Liam.

'Exactly!' said Lizzie, shooting him a grateful look that he'd come to that same conclusion quite so quickly and matter-of-factly.

'So... what's your plan?' he asked in amusement. 'You're going to shove them both in a beach hut?'

'Not quite,' said Lizzie shaking her head, 'but not too far off! I've got that big space outside the cottage, and if I could get my hands on a caravan – just for the short time the pair of them are with me – that could be the answer! I bet I could hire one from somewhere... and it's got to be cheaper than staying at the hotel while they're here!'

Liam stared at her silently for a moment, chewing on his lip, and Lizzie started to fidget. Why on earth did she have to go and mention the hotel? Now all she could think about was Liam in a fluffy robe!

'Tell you what,' said Liam at long last, 'you help me with the rest of these blasted chairs... and I reckon I might just have an idea!'

CHAPTER 13

Lizzie picked at her cuff. She was wearing her favourite yellow jumper under her trusty dungarees – but at this rate, she was going to shred it to pieces if she wasn't careful.

No – she absolutely hadn't dressed up just because Liam was on his way over to the cottage to pick her up. Nope – not at all… that would just be sad.

'Shut up, Lizzie!' she muttered to herself.

This wasn't her. She was calm… collected… allegedly cool! She didn't get worked up about such mundane things as collecting a caravan with her new… new… what, exactly? Friend she'd managed to accidentally bump faces with?

Catchy!

Lizzie sucked in a deep breath in a bid to calm herself down. She knew what the problem was, of course... this morning, it was a case of Liam to the rescue yet again. She hated feeling like she was a burden and she couldn't help but feel more than a little bit bad about dragging him out on yet another mission.

That said, the man simply wouldn't take "no" for an answer... which was just as well if she was being completely honest. Even if she could find her car keys in the disaster zone that was the half-tidied cottage, there was no way her little car would cope with towing a caravan along the narrow Seabury lanes.

Still... it meant accepting yet another favour from Liam, and Lizzie couldn't help the fact that she was struggling a bit when it came to embracing the damsel in distress vibes. Hence the dungarees and favourite jumper. This was what she wore when she wanted to feel more like herself - comfortable and capable and not even slightly in need of rescuing.

Lizzie still couldn't quite believe that Liam had managed to magic up a caravan for her to borrow with just a couple of phone calls. Yet again, the solution to her problem had started with Ted and Margie Hatherleigh - who she was quickly starting to view as her fairy god-grumps.

As it turned out, the caravan Margie wanted to buy needed to be moved from its current owners' yard asap as there was some muttering about it being sold to a dealer. As the Hatherleigh's lane needed a fair bit of work before they'd even be able to think about fitting a caravan down there, Liam had easily managed to convince both parties for Lizzie to borrow it for a couple of weeks. Suddenly, everyone was happy - Margie wouldn't miss out on her caravan, Mrs Watkins would see the back of it at long last, and Lizzie would have a bit more space while the girls were in town.

Lizzie took a deep breath as she watched Liam's van trundle towards her. Her treacherous heart had started to do annoying little backflips every time she set eyes on him. She plunged her hands into the pockets of her dungarees and dug the toe of her heavy boots into the compacted mud of the driveway. She was about as awkward as any fifteen-year-old waiting to be picked up for a date... and this *wasn't* a date. Not by a long shot. Lizzie didn't *do* dates!

As the van got closer, Lizzie spotted a familiar, furry face sitting next to Liam.

'Hello, you two!' she said as they pulled up next to her.

'Hey!' said Liam. 'Hope you don't mind, but Stanley decided he wanted to come for a ride. I stopped by The Sardine to grab us a takeaway coffee and the next thing I knew, he'd hopped up into the van!'

'Of course I don't!' said Lizzie, grinning at Stanley's panting face. 'Won't Ethel mind though? Or Sarah?'

'Nah,' said Liam, shaking his head. 'Sarah's at college today, and Ethel and Lou are run off their feet in the café. Ethel actually said it would be a relief not to have to worry about him making a break for it and going for a swim while they weren't looking! The courtyard was packed, and Stanley kept nipping out every time one of the visitors opened the door.'

'You're a monkey,' said Lizzie, scruffing Stanley's head as she climbed up next to him, getting a big, wet nose in her ear in the process.

'Right… let's go fetch this caravan!' said Liam, expertly manoeuvring the van so they were heading back towards the town. 'I think Mr and Mrs Watkins are thoroughly excited to see the back of the thing! They've got big plans for the bit of garden it's parked on, apparently.'

'Like what?' said Lizzie, settling back and smiling as she felt Stanley lean his entire weight against her side.

'Well… Mrs Watkins wants a conservatory, but from what I could make out, Mr Watkins fancies a trampoline… supposedly for the grandkids.'

Lizzie grinned. 'A bit of trampolining can't hurt!'

'Well… it can when you're in your eighties and you're already rocking a plastic knee,' laughed Liam as they made their way up the hill past the allotments.

'Okay, you might have a point there,' said Lizzie.

'Yep… I've got a feeling Mrs Watkins is going to win this particular battle!' he said. 'You're coffee's down there in the door by the way.'

∽

'I seriously can't believe how nice it is!' said Lizzie, peering in the passenger wing mirror to take another peep at the smart little caravan that was trundling along merrily behind the van.

For some reason, she'd been expecting a rusty shed on wheels – something with moss growing in the seams and dandelions sprouting along the narrow window ledges... but it was pristine.

Mrs Watkins had shown her where to find all the nifty storage spaces, where everything was tucked away in the tiny but perfectly formed kitchen, and how the dining table folded down into a double bed if the single bunk wasn't quite big enough.

'Yeah,' said Liam, 'they've definitely looked after it. I can see why Margie's so keen to get her hands on it.' He shot a look at Stanley, who was now flopped down between them, fast asleep with his head in Lizzie's lap. He'd had a grand time chasing after cheeky rabbits in the Watkins's garden. 'Do you think it'll make things easier when the girls turn up?'

'Definitely!' said Lizzie with a nod. 'In fact, the state the cottage is in at the moment, I think the three of us will be fighting it out as to who gets to stay in it!'

Liam laughed. 'Well good. I'm glad – and not bad going... two disasters averted in as many days!'

'Yeah,' said Lizzie, feeling suddenly awkward. 'Thanks so much. You've been really kind.'

'Ah, get away with you!' said Liam with a shrug. 'I

just happened to know the right people to point you at, that's all.'

'Erm... it's a bit more than that!' said Lizzie. 'I'm really grateful.'

'It's just what friends do,' he said, sounding awkward.

Lizzie raised her eyebrows.

Friends. Right.

Suddenly, she was thinking about that accidental kiss again. Neither of them had mentioned it... and now it would just be weird to bring it up. Still, a tiny splinter of disappointment had just lodged in her stomach when he'd dropped the "F" word so casually. Which was completely ridiculous. They *were* friends... and she should be grateful to have such a good friend so soon after moving back to town.

'Hey... I don't suppose I can tempt you to join me for a meal in The Pebble Street Hotel sometime?' she said, the words tumbling out before she could stop them. 'I mean... just to say thank you for everything!' she added quickly. 'I really want to find out what the food's like...'

Liam glanced at her, and Stanley stood up too, turning to stare at her with his eyebrows quivering.

Lizzie let out an uncomfortable laugh.

'What... you mean like a date?' said Liam.

Stanley turned to eyeball him.

'No!' said Lizzie quickly, feeling a blush hit her full force in the face. 'Not a date... I mean... just a-' she broke off as Stanley turned back to her and gave her a judgmental frown.

'It's a date!' said Liam.

'No... really - it isn't,' persisted Lizzie, doing her best not to laugh at the ridiculous dog, who now looked like he was watching a very slow tennis match as his head bobbed back and forth between them. 'More like a thank you, that's all.'

'Sounds like a date to me!' said Liam.

'You're impossible!' said Lizzie. 'It's *not* a date.'

'Can I wear my shorts?' he said.

'No,' said Lizzie.

'See – that makes it a date!'

'Honestly, men!' spluttered Lizzie.

Stanley let out a little *woof* of protest, and she snorted with laughter.

'Right... onto scarier things,' said Liam, as he turned down the lane that led towards her cottage.

'Uh oh,' said Lizzie, 'that sounds ominous.'

'I just mean reversing this monster into the right spot for you!' said Liam. 'Can you direct for me?'

'Sure!' said Lizzie with a shrug.

Liam came to a halt a little way from her drive, and she hopped down – making sure that Stanley stayed safely in the cab. All she needed to do was give Liam the heads up if he got too close to the ditch on one side or the hedge on the other – but as long as he kept it straight to start with, he shouldn't have any problems.

Two minutes later, Lizzie had broken into a cold

sweat at the number of times Liam had nearly lost a wheel into the ditch. He'd come very close to taking a chunk out of the hedge several times too!

'THE OTHER LEFT!' she yelled, wheeling her arms frantically in the air. Every move he made seemed to be making matters worse.

Liam came to a halt and she heard the handbrake going on. Hurrying to the window, she peered in.

'You okay?' she said.

'Sorry!' laughed Liam. 'I'm making a total hash of this. My brain doesn't like working in backwards mode at the best of times... especially not when I'm towing anything.'

'Why didn't you say something?' said Lizzie, raising her eyebrows.

'Erm... I've not tried it for ages... and I thought I might have miraculously got better somehow?'

'Right,' said Lizzie. 'Switch places! All I need you to do is give me a sign if I get closer than about a foot to the ditch, okay?'

She was half expecting Liam to protest. That's what Mark had always done. If it had anything to do with driving... or fixing things... or decorating... or washing the car... he'd always wanted to take the lead - even though he was totally crap when it came to anything practical. It was just a simple fact that out of the pair of them, she was the one with the practical brain, had a knack for fixing things and genuinely enjoyed doing it.

To his credit, Liam didn't even hesitate. In fact, a look of pure relief crossed his face as he hopped gleefully down to make way for her behind the steering wheel.

'Right boy, let's get this job done,' said Lizzie, putting the van into reverse, adjusting both the rear-view mirror and the wing-mirror on her side, before making sure that Liam was nice and visible.

One minute later, she had the caravan sitting neatly outside the cottage - exactly where she wanted it. Leaving the van running, she hopped down and moved around the back to help Liam with the tow-hitch.

'Okay... that was officially impressive!' he said, grinning at her.

'Nah!' said Lizzie. 'I'm just one of the lucky ones whose brain works well in reverse.'

'Well, I'm jealous!' said Liam. 'And relieved! That was getting embarrassing. It's always the way when you're trying to impress someone!'

Lizzie straightened up and was amused to see that the cool, unrufflable Liam was blushing. He clearly hadn't meant to say that last bit out loud.

'Anyway,' he muttered, making a beeline for the driver's seat again. 'I'd better be going. Lots to do!'

'Okay!' said Lizzie in surprise. She'd been half-hoping to talk him into a cuppa before he left. Instead, she watched as he quickly clambered back into the van. 'Well, thanks again. I'll book that table at the hotel, shall I?'

Liam nodded. 'For our date!'

Then he put his foot down and took off, leaving Lizzie staring at the back of the van as it disappeared down the lane.

'It's *not* a date!' she said to no one in particular.

CHAPTER 14

Considering tonight *definitely wasn't a date,* Lizzie was finding it ridiculously hard to choose what to wear for her meal with Liam. The minute he'd zoomed off after delivering the caravan, Lizzie had dashed inside to call the hotel and book a table before she chickened out of the whole thing.

As luck would have it, it was Lou who'd answered. As even *more* luck would have it, someone had just cancelled a table for two for the next night.

'It's perfect for a date,' Lou had added, with a definite smirk in her voice.

With much awkward spluttering, Lizzie had firmed up the booking, and done her best to dodge Lou's inquisitive questioning (otherwise known as the third-degree). In the end, she'd simply given in and told her that she was treating Liam to a meal to say thank you for all his help.

'Like a date?' Lou had said.

'Definitely *not* a date!' Lizzie had replied firmly.

Now, though – with the huge laundry bags containing her clothes upended all over the living room while she tried on outfit after outfit – even Lizzie had to admit to herself that it was starting to feel a *lot* like a date.

Still, it wasn't a crime to want to look her best, was it? Plus, it gave her a great excuse to unpack her clothes. Lizzie really wished she'd just binned half of these things before she'd moved. Instead, she'd followed the path of least resistance and bunged them into the huge tartan bags with a promise to herself that she'd have a proper clear out once she'd settled in.

Picking up something pink and sparkly, Lizzie frowned, absolutely convinced it wasn't hers. It wasn't that she had anything against pink… or sparkles come to that… but she'd never actively choose to wear either!

'Oh my god!' she laughed, holding up the tent-like smock in front of her.

How on earth had she managed to keep this for so long? It was a maternity top her old nan had given her when Megan was little more than a bump. She couldn't remember ever actually wearing it – favouring voluminous men's shirts of ever-increasing sizes instead – but because it had come from her nan, she'd never had the heart to get rid of it.

'Well, I'm not wearing you!' she laughed, tossing it

over the back of the sofa and staring forlornly at the heap in front of her.

This was ridiculous. Shouldn't she just pick whatever she was most comfortable in and settle for that? A pair of dungarees would definitely make life easier – she could change things up a bit and go for her bottle-green, cropped cord ones for a change? But no – that wasn't fair on Liam after she'd banned him from wearing shorts!

A little flutter of nerves hit Lizzie in the chest and she straightened up for a moment, taking a deep breath. At least he wasn't coming to the cottage to pick her up – that would have been excruciating! Even if Liam *did* want to go in for anything quite so soppy, there was no way they could arrange it because she didn't even have his mobile number. In fact... she wasn't sure if he'd turn up at all!

Lizzie had left a note pinned to the door of the deckchair hut with their booking time, and then she'd left a message for him in The Sardine for good measure – asking him to meet her at the hotel. Then she'd spent all day with her eyes peeled, hoping to bump into him... but typically, he seemed to have vanished into thin air.

Blowing out a long breath in an attempt to calm herself down, Lizzie shrugged. There was nothing she could do about it now. She'd just have to hope that he'd got the message... and was able to come!

'What's the worst-case scenario?' she muttered, rooting around in the pile of clothes again.

Well... that was easy enough to answer. If Liam didn't turn up she'd just have to sit at her table for two like Billy-no-mates and enjoy a meal for one instead. Frankly, on a normal day, that wouldn't bother her in the slightest. If it happened tonight though – she had to admit she'd be pretty gutted. And something told her Lou probably wouldn't ever let her live it down, either!

'Think positive, woman!'

All being well, in just over an hour she'd be sharing a meal at a swanky restaurant with the cutest guy she'd set eyes on in... well... decades!

Okay... so... if this *was* a date... what would she wear? It had been a very long time since she'd even considered that question... but surely she could figure something out!

~

Pulling the front door of the cottage closed behind her, Lizzie took a deep breath, willing the butterflies in her chest to bog off. She knew she was being ridiculous – and frankly, this wasn't like her at all. She didn't go all gooey and silly... but right now she was doing just that.

Still, at least she'd finally found something to wear. Plus, one good thing had come out of turning the living room into a complete bomb site – she'd found her car keys at long last. They'd managed to get wedged down between the sofa cushions and, by a stroke of luck, they'd got tangled up in a cardigan sleeve and leapt out on her when she went to try it on.

Not that she was going to take the car this evening. For one thing, she wanted to have the option to help herself to a bit of Dutch courage if she needed it, and for another, she was already feeling way too giddy to be in charge of a vehicle. Hopefully – a nice breezy walk down to The Pebble Street Hotel should knock a bit of sense into her... and it would give her an excuse for looking a bit pink-cheeked and windswept when she got there too! Lizzie really did feel like a teenager again... silly, giddy and very alive. She had to admit, it felt pretty bloody wonderful.

Anyway, this was her last night of freedom. Both the girls were due to descend on Seabury the next day, and their arrival would shake everything up all over again... but Lizzie was looking forward to seeing them. Perhaps they'd get the chance to meet Liam while they were here. Not that he was her boyfriend... or her *anything* really, but... well... he *was* her friend, so that counted, didn't it?

For a moment, Lizzie's head filled with Liam as she wondered what the girls would make of him. They'd like him, of course – who wouldn't? It was hard not to, with his wild, tousled hair and his ever-present shorts and mischievous smile.

'Breathe!' she muttered, slowing down a bit as she

neared the seafront and the butterflies took flight again.

She paused in front of a little cottage, trying to catch a glimpse of her reflection in the window... just to check she still looked okay. Part of her wished she'd had the balls to go all-out and wear her little black dress... but that was *way* too try-hard for a casual meal with a friend. The other part of her wished she'd just stuck to her dungarees.

Instead, here she was, stuck in the middle somewhere, wearing her skinny black jeans and a cute black top that with its wide boat neck in a skull and crossbones print. She'd pulled her hair back with one of her red and white bandanas and even added a touch of red lippy. That was the bit she felt most uncomfortable about... but the over-excited teen that seemed to have body-snatched her had insisted. Still... at least she wasn't wearing heels. Her feet were comfy in her usual beaten-up old Converse.

Resisting the urge to grab a tissue and wipe off the lippy, Lizzie forced her steps onward towards the hotel. Why did this evening feel like it could be the start of something... new? Something... big? There was a strange weight of expectation around the whole thing.

'Urgh,' she groaned, stopping again when she came within sight of the hotel's front door. This had been a bad, bad idea. What if he didn't turn up? What if he hadn't got her messages?

He must have.

She'd left them all over town.

Lizzie willed herself to move forward and go inside the hotel, but she seemed to be rooted to the spot.

Why was this such a massive deal all of a sudden? This was just two friends meeting up for a casual meal. If Liam didn't turn up... it wasn't a big deal! Except it was. She'd be crushed!

Lizzie knew she was fooling herself – she knew exactly why this was so important to her. It was the first time she'd even bothered to look at another man since her divorce. In that time, Mark had moved on, dated and got married again. But she'd needed the time to grieve – not for her marriage - but for her little family unit that seemed to have dissolved overnight.

And now... she was ready to move on. She'd already taken huge steps to change her life into the one she wanted... but these little flutterings she felt every time she thought of Liam? They were new... and frankly, they were terrifying!

'Are you going to stand out there all night?'

The voice made Lizzie jump. She'd been gazing absently beyond the Pebble Street Hotel across the King's Nose, where the point jutted out to sea. Now her attention snapped back to the hotel. The door had been flung open and a face was grinning out at her. It had to be...

'Lou?' said Lizzie. 'I barely recognised you minus the swimming cap!'

'The one and only!' laughed Lou. 'I'll let you off... especially as you look a bit like someone's clonked you over the head this evening – you're in that much of a daze!'

Lizzie grinned at her. 'Yeah... just a bit preoccupied.'

'Well, don't get your knickers in a twist,' said Lou. 'Your date's here!'

'*Not* a date!' said Lizzie, even as she blew out a breath of pure relief.

'If it looks like a date and wiggles like a date, then it must be a date,' said Lou blandly. 'Besides – if it's not a date, why do you look quite so hot right now?!'

Lizzie's grin widened even as she felt her cheeks flame at the compliment. It was a very long time since anyone had told her she was hot... in fact, this might be the first time ever!

'Erm... thanks?' she said, feeling awkward.

'Just stating a fact,' Lou shrugged. 'Anyway, the question still stands... are you just going to hang around out here making poor Liam sweat, or are you going to come in and have something to eat?!'

'Oh!' said Lizzie. 'Right... yeah. I'm coming in.'

'Excellent,' said Lou with a wide smile. 'Follow me – I'll take you to your table.'

CHAPTER 15

Lizzie paused for just a second before following Lou through the gleaming doorway - she couldn't help taking a moment to admire the neatly clipped, narrow strip of front garden, polished menu holders, and neat welcome mat. The Pebble Street Hotel gleamed golden and welcoming in the evening air.

It was very different to what she remembered from when the girls were little and Veronica Hughes had ruled the roost. Then it had been scruffy, run-down and vastly overpriced.

'I know!' said Lou, grinning at Lizzie as she followed her into the foyer, only to stop again.

Okay – this was far beyond welcoming. This was stunning!

'Erm... so it's changed a bit in here, then!' said Lizzie, running a nervous hand down her top and skinny jeans. Clearly, a beaten-up pair of her favourite shoes had been a very poor choice. This place deserved designer heels at the very least!

The last time she'd been in here was when Jenna was tiny, and one of the mothers had booked the dining room for her son's birthday party. The poor woman was new in town, so it wasn't her fault that she'd inadvertently subjected the kids to an hour and a half of pure torture as they'd all sat quietly on sticky, grubby chairs, not daring to make a sound in case they invoked the wrath of Veronica.

'Lionel's done a gorgeous job, hasn't he?' said Lou. 'Just wait until you've tried the food too. Hattie's a genius.'

Lizzie shot her a nervous smile. She normally had the appetite of a horse, but she was so worked up right now, she had a feeling she'd struggle to eat a single bite.

'Right,' said Lou, tugging at her elbow, 'don't leave that poor guy waiting any longer. He's been here for ages.'

'Oh don't!' said Lizzie, pulling a face.

'Okay… ten minutes!' said Lou, shooting her a naughty wink.

Lizzie grinned back. She might not be quite in the right frame of mind to fully appreciate Lou's friendliness and banter, but she had a sneaking suspicion she might have just met a kindred spirit. Lou's smile was infectious, and she clearly didn't believe in taking life's little moments too seriously.

'Right... let me at him!' said Lizzie, blowing out a breath and squaring her shoulders.

'That's more like it!' said Lou approvingly.

Lizzie followed her new friend into a beautiful dining room. Parquet floor gleamed underfoot, and the cream-clothed tables were surrounded by merry-faced diners. Light spilled into the room from the wide doors at the far end, and Lizzie could suddenly see why the place had such a good reputation these days. If you were going to splash out on a nice meal, this was the perfect place to do it!

Considering it was still pretty early, the restaurant was already packed, and there was a lovely, light buzz of chatter in the air. As her eyes danced around the room, trying to take everything in, Lizzie spotted Liam at a cosy table for two near the windows. The minute he saw her, he got to his feet.

Lizzie let out a low gasp of pure appreciation.

'Scrubs up pretty well, eh?' breathed Lou over her shoulder as she led Lizzie towards the table.

Lizzie just widened her eyes. There was *no way* she was going to let the fact that she heartily agreed with Lou escape her lips. Not when she was this close to Liam, and the man in question seemed to have his eyes glued on her as she approached him.

'Hey!' he said as they came to a standstill next to his table.

Lou was beaming like a Cheshire cat as she stared from Lizzie to Liam and then back again.

'Hi,' said Lizzie, smiling at him nervously and doing her best to ignore the over-excited Lou, who was practically vibrating next to her.

'You look amazing,' said Liam.

'Aw!' said Lou with a squeak. 'Sorry... I mean... I'll leave you to your date.'

'It's not a date!' they both chorused as Lou scuttled away.

Lizzie turned an amused smile on Liam. 'Thanks, by the way. You look fab too.'

'No shorts, as promised,' he said with a shrug.

'Well... you look great,' she said awkwardly. Because he really did scrub up remarkably well. It wasn't like he was wearing a suit – thank heavens - but his dark blue shirt looked like it had seen an iron relatively recently, and he was wearing a pair of light chinos.

'Here,' he said, hurrying around to her side of the table and pulling her chair out for her.

'Thanks!' said Lizzie in surprise. As she sat down awkwardly, she got a waft of something woody and spicy and ridiculously delicious. Probably Liam's shower gel. The scent practically made her shiver. Blimey... considering this really *wasn't* a date, it was off to an excellent start.

'Want to hear something weird?' he said, grinning at her as he sat back down.

'Always!' she said, smiling at him and feeling some of her nerves start to melt away.

'I'm nervous,' he said, looking slightly sheepish. 'I've

been nervous ever since I picked up your message earlier.'

Lizzie smiled at him broadly. 'Yeah. Me too.'

'You?' said Liam in surprise, rubbing the back of his neck. 'I didn't think anything fazed you!'

'Are you kidding me?!' laughed Lizzie. 'Pretty much *everything* fazes me. You saw what I was like when I thought I might not be able to open the shop!'

'That's different,' said Liam quickly. 'That's your dream! And anyway – you were still super-cool about it all.'

'I think it was you who was cool – swooping in with a solution,' said Lizzie. 'And again with the caravan.'

'It was nothing,' said Liam. 'Both times!' he added with a laugh. 'Anyway – have you decided which one of the girls is going in there?'

'Probably Jenna,' said Lizzie, finally deciding that she couldn't possibly wait a single second longer to give into her grumbling stomach. It looked like her appetite was back with a vengeance. Liam seemed to be intent on ignoring the warm, herb-scented bread that was sitting in the basket between them, but there was no way she could last another second.

Choosing a roll, she ripped off a chunk and spread it with a thick layer of creamy butter.

'Though,' she said, glancing up at Liam, 'the caravan is such a nice space, I was serious when I said I might commandeer it for myself and leave those two to fight it out in the cottage!'

She took a bite of her bread and rolled her eyes, a small groan of pleasure escaping her lip.

'Okay, that's it!' laughed Liam, grabbing a roll for himself. 'I'm starving!'

'Me too!' said Lizzie.

'Good,' said Liam. 'In that case, shall I get Lou over and we'll get our orders in… and… from previous experience, I can recommend the Pebble Street pudding.'

'Shall we share one?' said Lizzie.

'Share?' said Liam. 'No. Definitely not. Or at least, not the first portion. I'd say we order three… one each and the third to share.'

'It's that good?' said Lizzie.

'You'd better believe it. Anyway, if you don't like it, I'll gladly clear up the extras!' said Liam.

'Right… in that case, you're on!' said Lizzie, turning to wave to Lou.

～

Lizzie leaned against the railings for a moment, letting the cool air from the sea dance across her pink cheeks. It had been an unexpectedly wonderful evening. Of course – she should have known it would be fun because Liam was such easy company. But… this had been more than fun.

Their cosy table had been like a private little island – a bubble that contained just the two of them. After the initial awkwardness had passed, the pair of them chatted away as though the rest of the diners didn't even exist. In fact... three hours later and they really *didn't* exist – the pair of them had closed the restaurant... even though Lizzie could swear the entire meal had only lasted ten minutes.

In the end, it had taken some seriously heavy hinting from Lou about her tired feet and the fact that were already on their third coffee to get them to pay up and leave. Lizzie made sure she left a generous tip... and she had a feeling Lou would be in touch for all the gossip tomorrow anyway!

Lizzie closed her eyes for just a moment, relishing the memory of every time their knees had touched under the table... and that moment Liam had reached across and rested his hand on hers... just for a moment. It had felt like the most intimate, exciting thing that had ever happened to her.

But... as with all good things, it had come to an end. She had the long walk back up to the cottage, and Liam needed to head back to his own place... wherever that was.

'Okay – slightly awkward question,' she said, turning to face him and watching as he pulled on his jacket.

'O-kay?' said Liam.

'Where do you live?!' she said.

'How very forward!' he said, his eyebrows shooting up in mock surprise.

Lizzie stuck her tongue out at him, her pleasant, wine-haze leading the way. 'I didn't mean that!' she laughed. 'I just meant – are we walking together for a bit or are you in the other direction?'

'And why's that awkward?' he said curiously.

'Because you know nearly everything about me – where I live, why I'm back, why I'm divorced… you know all about the girls arriving… and helped me to find somewhere for them to stay… and I don't even know where you live!'

'Oh!' said Liam. 'Well, I'm on Sand Piper Lane. But I'm walking you back up to your cottage first. It's far too late for wandering around the lanes on your own!'

'This is Seabury!' said Lizzie with a shrug.

'I don't care,' said Liam. 'Don't worry, I'll be a gent. I won't even come through the garden gate.'

'Shame,' said Lizzie, then promptly clapped a hand over her mouth.

'Lizzie Moore!' he laughed. 'I thought this wasn't a date?'

Lizzie cocked her head, staring at him for a moment. 'It's not,' she said, pushing away from the barriers and moving slowly towards him. 'But not because I don't want it to be.'

'Oh?' said Liam, his eyes widening slightly as she came to stand right in front of him.

She looked down, making sure her Converse were toe to toe with his boots.

'So…' he said quietly when she looked at him. 'So… why isn't it a date again?'

'Because,' said Lizzie, 'I quite like the idea of another – official - first date.'

'You do?' said Liam.

'I do,' she said, holding his gaze. His eyes were a soft grey, but this close, she could see the dark, navy ring around his irises. 'What about you?'

'Me?' said Liam. 'I think I'd like to kiss you right now.'

'Here?' breathed Lizzie.

Liam nodded.

'Okay!' said Lizzie, her heart going into overdrive even as the most ridiculous smile spread across her lips. She stared at him, and he stared right back, not moving. Lizzie shrugged, and leaning in, she kissed him very lightly on the corner of the mouth before stepping back, still smiling.

'Coming?' she said, holding out her hand.

Liam nodded and, reaching out, threaded his fingers through hers.

Warmth seemed to spread up her arm as the pair of them wandered along the seafront hand in hand in complete silence.

They only got as far as The Sardine before Liam drew her towards him. Smoothing her hair away from her face with his free hand, he kissed her under the street light.

CHAPTER 16

All Lizzie really wanted to do right now was spend the morning lazing around in bed... but as much as she'd love nothing more than to curl up with the duvet and imagine it was Liam's arms wrapped around her, she really had to get up.

Today was the day she had to pick both the girls up from the train station in Plymouth. By some complete fluke, they were arriving on the same train... though typically, they'd managed to book seats at opposite ends of the thing!

Lizzie knew she should be over the moon about seeing them. This was her chance for some quality family time – a rare thing these days! Right now, though, all she wanted to do was re-live the night before.

Liam had walked her all the way home – and just as he'd promised, he hadn't even set foot inside the garden gate. That didn't mean they hadn't kissed like teenagers all the way up the hill from town, though.

It must have taken them over an hour to reach the cottage, and then they'd stayed outside for ages, snogging against the side of the caravan. It had taken every last drop of Lizzie's willpower not to drag Liam inside when she'd finally retreated into the cottage. Now wasn't the time to rush things, though. She wanted to savour every last second of whatever this was.

Considering it hadn't been a date, it had been pretty bloody wonderful! Lizzie shivered and curled her toes at the thought. Who was she kidding? Of *course* last night had been a date. One of the best dates she'd ever had, in fact. Even so, she couldn't wait to see what came next. Liam had promised her that their *official* first date would be special. All she knew was that it was going to have to go some to beat last night!

Sadly though, all that was going to have to wait.

Glancing at the clock on her bedside table, Lizzie realised that she needed to get a wiggle on. There were still a few boxes in her car left over from the move, and she needed to drop them off at the Old Grain Store before heading to Plymouth – otherwise there wouldn't be enough in there for the girls and their bags!

With a groan, Lizzie pushed the duvet back and clambered out of bed. She needed at least two buckets of coffee before it was time to go. All that kissing might have made her feel like a randy teenager – but her ability to deal with late nights definitely hadn't got the memo.

~

Lizzie was just emerging from the Old Grain Store when Liam's van appeared, heading in her direction. She grinned as he slowed down.

'I enjoyed our date!' he shouted out of the window as he trundled past.

'It wasn't a date!' she called back, laughing as he disappeared towards North Beach. 'Idiot!' she added with a giggle.

It wasn't long before she was ensconced in her own car and heading out of town in the opposite direction, wishing that she could spend some time with Liam later on. There was no way she was about to abandon the girls the moment they got here, though!

Lizzie sighed. She wasn't entirely sure when they'd be able to grab some time alone together, but they'd work something out.

'Get a grip!' she chuckled.

It was like the man had somehow managed to set up camp in her head. She blamed those kisses... especially the ones where he'd pressed her up against the side of the caravan!

Good grief!

'Maybe not while you're driving!' she gasped, winding the window down so that she could get some fresh air. The little car seemed to be incredibly warm all of a sudden!

The drive to the station didn't seem to take as long as usual... but perhaps that was because her mind was full of her new boyfriend.

Boyfriend!

That might be taking things a little bit too far! Liam was definitely *not* a boy. Boys didn't kiss like that.

Blimey!

Maybe it was a good thing the girls were about to descend on her after all. This really was the last thing she'd been expecting when she'd moved back to Seabury, and she could do without completely losing her head over the poor guy! Even so, she had to admit that the previous evening had been... exciting. Stupidly, wonderfully exciting. She couldn't wait to do it all over again as soon as she could pin Liam down.

That was possibly the worst choice of words she could have gone with... and they'd made her all hot and bothered again. Lizzie rolled her eyes at herself, fanning her face with her hand.

Right... it was time to go and meet the girls... and push all sordid thoughts out of her head while she was at it!

Lizzie managed to reach the platform just as the train doors were opening, and a swoop of excitement ran through her. It might have presented her with a bit of a logistical nightmare, but having her little family all back under the same roof was going to be wonderful.

Well... kind of under the same roof... and Mark wouldn't be joining them, would he? But... that was okay!

Suddenly, after all these years, it really *was* okay. Mark would always be her friend, but the dark hole in her heart that had been reserved for them as a couple had miraculously disappeared. In its place was a huge bubble of gratitude – for Seabury, for her new friends and new business... and for the possibility of something else new... hinted at by an entire evening of stolen kisses.

As the commuters started to stream from the train, their heads down, eyes glued to their phones like a hoard of zombies, Lizzie stared around, trying to catch sight of the girls.

'Jenna!' she yelled, raising her hand in the air to catch the attention of her youngest as she stepped down from the train. Jenna's face creased into a wide smile, and pushing her mane of tangled, strawberry blond hair over one shoulder, she floated in Lizzie's direction.

Lizzie couldn't help but smile. With her long white cotton dress and patchwork jacket, Jenna stood out like a beacon against the rest of the passengers. Even though she'd been travelling for hours and must be stressed out of her brain, she looked relaxed and happy. Her eyes glittered with life as she dumped her bags onto the ground and threw her arms around Lizzie in a tight hug.

'Yay! Mum!' she squealed, right in her ear.

Lizzie grinned, sinking into Jenna's embrace for a moment, only to let out a little cough and step back quickly.

'Sorry,' laughed Jenna. 'Everything about me smells like burning van!'

Lizzie nodded, wriggling her nose, trying to rid herself of the weird scent of burning electrics.

'Meggie!' squealed Jenna, almost bursting Lizzie's eardrums in the process.

Sure enough, there was Megan... but not the Megan she remembered from their last catch-up over coffee in Bristol. Her eldest daughter looked like she'd deflated somehow. Her usually immaculate dark bob was lifeless, flat and pulled back behind her ears. Megan wasn't wearing a scrap of makeup – not a bad thing in itself, but Lizzie didn't think she'd seen Megan's bare face since she was about thirteen.

Also missing in action was the usual sharp blazer, neat pencil skirt and ballet pumps. Instead, Megan was wearing a tired old pair of jogging trousers, battered trainers and a motheaten sweatshirt with a glittery cat on the front. Lizzie frowned. She recognized that cat – she'd bought it for Megan as a joke when she was about sixteen. Her daughter had been horrified. The fact she was wearing it now didn't bode well.

'Don't call me that,' Megan grouched as she made her way over to her little sister.

Lizzie smiled. She might not look like her old self

right now, but that response was classic, old-school Megan.

'Why not, Meggie-Moo?' said Jenna with a beatific smile as she wrapped her arm around her sister's neck in a hug that was nearing head-lock territory.

'Get off!' said Megan, struggling to break free whilst completely failing to keep a tired smile off her face as Jenna planted a sloppy kiss on her temple.

'Hi love,' said Lizzie, stepping forward to give her daughter a hug. It was nothing like the all-enveloping cuddle she'd just received from Jenna. A quick double pat on the back before she was pushed away again.

'Jeez mum, what are you wearing?!' said Megan, staring in mild horror at Lizzie's cord dungarees.

'I think you'll find she looks fabulous!' said Jenna enthusiastically. 'Whereas you look like...'

'*Girls! Quit it!*' said Lizzie, sensing a quarrel brewing at ten paces. They weren't even in the car yet... it wasn't a good omen for what the few weeks were going to be like! Any hope she had that the girls might rub along a bit better now that they were older promptly disappeared.

'Can we get going?' said Megan. 'I'm knackered.'

'*You're* knackered?!' laughed Jenna. 'I'm the one who's been on all the planes in the entire world!'

'Don't exaggerate!' huffed Megan. 'Anyway – it's not our fault you haven't got an ounce of ambition and keep disappearing all over the place.'

Lizzie rolled her eyes and decided that she didn't

have the energy to step in between them again. She grabbed Megan's large suitcase – ominously heavy considering she'd said she'd only be staying for a couple of days - and started to lead the way back to the car.

'Shotgun!' said Jenna, the moment they reached it.

'No way, I'm sitting up front,' said Megan. 'I'm the one that gets car-sick.'

'Give over,' said Jenna. 'You've not been car-sick since you were eight – and that's only because you stuffed your face with too much candyfloss and then went on the big wheel!'

Lizzie grimaced. She remembered that journey far too well, even though it had been Mark who'd cleared up the violent pink puddles from the back of the passenger seat!

'Anyway,' said Jenna, 'I've been away for longer and I want to tell mum about the van blowing up.'

'No way – I-'

'You can *both* sit in the back!' said Lizzie, quickly pulling rank before the girls descended into all-out war in the car park.

While the pair of them muttered and mumbled their way into the back seat, with plenty of elbowing on the way in, Lizzie hefted the big case into the front seat and buckled it in. At least it wasn't Jenna's case... though she could already smell the fumes wafting towards her from the boot. Something told her that her little car would always have a slight whiff of burning van from now on.

Lizzie barely had to say a word all the way back to Seabury – the girls were too intent on quarrelling about every single little thing. She was just turning down the lane that led down into the town when she remembered something.

'Have either of you heard from your dad yet?' she said, shooting a quick look in the rear-view mirror. She caught a look pass between them that she didn't quite understand.

'Nope,' said Jenna.

'Me neither,' said Megan.

'I'm a bit worried,' said Jenna.

'Yeah...' said Megan.

Lizzie bit her lip. She knew it had precisely nothing to do with her these days, but the fact that Mark hadn't messaged either of the girls or returned their calls was definitely odd.

'Well... shall we try him again over the weekend?' she said.

'Yeah,' said Megan. 'I've left about a dozen messages, but he's not even seen some of them.'

Lizzie frowned. 'Erm... either of you tried calling Tiffany?'

'Hell no!' laughed Jenna.

Megan shook her head.

'Right... well, maybe that would be a good plan?' she suggested.

'Can you do it?' said Jenna.

Seriously? She hadn't signed up for calling her ex-husband's new wife just because he'd gone incommunicado. But then... she *was* starting to get a bit worried.

'Let's see if we can get hold of him... if not, then we'll call Tiff.'

'Eww!' said Jenna.

Lizzie smirked. Her daughter's sentiment just about covered it.

'Right!' said Lizzie, 'here we are!'

She slowed the car down, ready to pull up next to the caravan.

'Mother,' said Megan, 'what the *hell* is that?!'

'Cool!' said Jenna.

'That... is going to be a bedroom for one of you,' said Lizzie, bracing for the storm of complaints.

'Me!' said Megan.

'No – me!' said Jenna.

'I asked first,' said Megan.

Lizzie let out a sigh, killed the engine and hopped out of the car. She needed coffee. She'd leave those two to fight it out between them.

'Take a look before ripping each other's hair out,' she laughed before making her way towards the cottage. 'I'll put the kettle on.'

'But mum...' said Jenna.

'If my case is in there, it's mine!' crowed Megan.

Lizzie closed her eyes briefly, wondering how she'd

somehow managed to travel back in time during the drive back from Plymouth.

Coffee – that was the only answer – before she started to tear her hair out. She pushed her way through the garden gate and then broke into a wide smile.

There, leaning against the front door, was a beautiful bunch of wildflowers, tied together with what looked like a piece of old deck-chair fabric.

Suddenly, Lizzie was firmly back in the present. Even if her daughters were squabbling behind like they were back in primary school… Lizzie was ready to stride into her future - and it was bright and full of first dates and toe-curling kisses.

THE END

Head back to Seabury and catch part two of Lizzie's story with ***In A Spin in Seabury***

ALSO BY BETH RAIN

Seabury Series:

Welcome to Seabury (Seabury Book 1)

Trouble in Seabury (Seabury Book 2)

Christmas in Seabury (Seabury Book 3)

Sandwiches in Seabury (Seabury Book 4)

Secrets in Seabury (Seabury Book 5)

Surprises in Seabury (Seabury Book 6)

Dreams and Ice Creams in Seabury (Seabury Book 7)

Mistakes and Heartbreaks in Seabury (Seabury Book 8)

Laughter and Happy Ever After in Seabury (Seabury Book 9)

A Quiet Life in Seabury (Seabury Book 10)

In A Spin in Seabury (Seabury Book 11)

Living The Dream in Seabury (Seabury Book 12)

A Big Day in Seabury (Seabury Book 13)

Something Borrowed in Seabury (Seabury Book 14)

A Match Made in Seabury (Seabury Book 15)

Seabury Series Collections:

Kate's Story: Books 1 - 3

Hattie's Story: Books 4 - 6

Standalones: Books 7 - 9

Lizzie's Story: Books 10 - 12

Upper Bamton Series:

Upper Bamton: The Complete Series Collection: Books 1 - 4

Individual titles:

A New Arrival in Upper Bamton (Upper Bamton Book 1)

Rainy Days in Upper Bamton (Upper Bamton Book 2)

Hidden Treasures in Upper Bamton (Upper Bamton Book 3)

Time Flies By in Upper Bamton (Upper Bamton Book 4)

Standalone Books:

How to be Angry at Christmas

Crumbleton Series:

Coming Home to Crumbleton (Crumbleton Book 1)

Flowers Go Flying in Crumbleton (Crumbleton Book 2)

Match Point in Crumbleton (Crumbleton Book 3)

A Very Crumbleton Christmas (Crumbleton Book 4)

Little Bamton Series:

Little Bamton: The Complete Series Collection: Books 1 - 5

Individual titles:

Christmas Lights and Snowball Fights (Little Bamton Book 1)

Spring Flowers and April Showers (Little Bamton Book 2)

Summer Nights and Pillow Fights (Little Bamton Book 3)

Autumn Cuddles and Muddy Puddles (Little Bamton Book 4)

Christmas Flings and Wedding Rings (Little Bamton Book 5)

Crumcarey Island Series:

Crumcarey Island Series Collection: Books 1 - 5

Individual titles:

Christmas on Crumcarey (Crumcarey Island Book 1)

All Change on Crumcarey (Crumcarey Island Book 2)

Making Waves on Crumcarey (Crumcarey Island Book 3)

Fool's Gold on Crumcarey (Crumcarey Island Book 4)

A Fresh Start on Crumcarey (Crumcarey Island Book 5)

WRITING AS BEA FOX

What's a Girl To Do? The Complete Series

Individual titles:

The Holiday: What's a Girl To Do? (Book 1)

The Wedding: What's a Girl To Do? (Book 2)

The Lookalike: What's a Girl To Do? (Book 3)

The Reunion: What's a Girl To Do? (Book 4)

At Christmas: What's a Girl To Do? (Book 5)

ABOUT THE AUTHOR

Beth Rain has always wanted to be a writer and has been penning adventures for characters ever since she learned to stare into the middle-distance and daydream.

She recently moved to a windswept, Scottish island, and it is a dream come true to spend her days hanging out with Bob – her trusty laptop – scoffing crisps and chocolate while dreaming up swoony love stories for all her imaginary friends.

Beth's writing will always deliver on the happy-ever-afters, so if you need cosy… you're in safe hands!

Visit www.bethrain.com for all the bookish goodness and keep up with all Beth's news by joining her newsletter!

facebook.com/BethRainBooks
twitter.com/bethrainauthor
instagram.com/bethrainauthor

Printed in Dunstable, United Kingdom